The Dog
Who Thought
He Was
Santa

Books by Bill Wallace

The Backward Bird Dog
Beauty
The Biggest Klutz of Fifth Grade
Blackwater Swamp
Buffalo Gal
The Christmas Spurs
Coyote Autumn
Danger in Quicksand Swamp
Danger on Panther Peak
   [Original title: Shadow on the Snow]
A Dog Called Kitty
The Dog Who Thought He Was Santa
Eye of the Great Bear
Ferret in the Bedroom, Lizards in
   the Fridge
The Final Freedom
Journey into Terror
The Ledgend of Thunderfoot
Never Say Quit
No Dogs Allowed!
The Pick of the Litter
Red Dog
Skinny-Dipping at Monster Lake
Snot Stew
Totally Disgusting!
Trapped in Death Cave
True Friends
Upchuck and the Rotten Willy
Upchuck and the Rotten Willy:
   The Great Escape
Upchuck and the Rotten Willy:
   Running Wild
Watchdog and the Coyotes

Books by Carol and Bill Wallace

The Flying Flea, Callie, and Me
That Furball Puppy and Me
Chomps, Flea, and Gray Cat
   (That's Me!)
Bub Moose
Bub, Snow, and the Burly Bear
   Scare
The Meanest Hound Around

Books by Nikki Wallace

Stubby and the Puppy Pack
Stubby and the Puppy Pack to
   the Rescue

AVAILABLE FROM
SIMON & SCHUSTER

The Dog
Who Thought
He Was
Santa

by

Bill Wallace

ALADDIN PAPERBACKS
NEW YORK   LONDON   TORONTO   SYDNEY

This book is a work of fiction. Any references to historical events, real people, or real locales are used fictitiously. Other names, characters, places, and incidents are the product of the author's imagination, and any resemblance to actual events or locales or persons, living or dead, is entirely coincidental.

ALADDIN PAPERBACKS
An imprint of Simon & Schuster Children's Publishing Division
1230 Avenue of the Americas, New York, NY 10020
Copyright © 2007 by Bill Wallace
Published by arrangement with Holiday House, Inc.
All rights reserved, including the right of reproduction in whole or in part in any form.
For information contact Holiday House, 425 Madison Avenue, New York, NY 10017
ALADDIN PAPERBACKS and related logo are registered trademarks of
Simon & Schuster, Inc.
Manufactured in the United States of America
First Aladdin Paperbacks edition October 2008
2 4 6 8 10 9 7 5 3 1
The Library of Congress has cataloged the hardcover edition as follows:
Wallace, Bill, 1947–
The dog who thought he was Santa / by Bill Wallace.—1st ed.
Summary: In 1957, problems at the mine threaten to ruin Christmas for fifth-grader Don, his family, and the rest of their Oklahoma coal town, but Don's bloodhound, Frank, is determined to do whatever it takes to make the holiday special for Don and his six-year-old sister, Susan. Alternate chapters are told from the human and canine points of view.
[1. Family life—Oklahoma—Fiction. 2. Bloodhound—Fiction.
3. Dogs—Fiction. 4. Coal mines and mining—Fiction. 5. Christmas—Fiction.
6. Oklahoma—History—20th century—Fiction.] I. Title.
PZ7.W15473 Dog 2007
[Fic]—dc22
2007021733
ISBN-13: 978-1-4169-4816-2 (pbk)
ISBN-10: 1-4169-4816-3 (pbk)

To Jon-Ed Moore,
our son-in-law,
who wanted a book dedicated to him
where the dog doesn't die

Chapter

1

Don Franklin jumped when he realized that half the kids in his fifth-grade room were already out the door.

He hadn't even heard the bell.

Like the rest of his class, Don had watched the clock from noon on. The closer it got to three thirty, the slower its hands seemed to move. As long as his eyes were on the clock, he was able to keep the thoughts—the worry—from his mind. But when he looked away—when he even so much as tried *not* to think—the thoughts snared him like the thin strands of a spider's web.

Realizing he might be the last one to leave for Christmas vacation, he leaped out of his chair and glanced around to see what he needed to carry home. *No homework,* he thought with a smile, *and two weeks off. All I need is my coat.*

When he'd left the house this morning, his dad had said he wouldn't need his coat; but his mom made him take it anyway. When it came to weather, his dad always knew what to expect—everyone in Devlin Hollow knew that. But Don did what his mom told him to do.

Since it was so warm, he tied the coat sleeves loosely around his waist and took off. He didn't pause to visit with anyone. Didn't scuffle with Kyle Benson on the way to the parking lot. He just headed to the bus.

Part of his excitement was happy, on account of getting out of school for Christmas. Part was hopeful—hopeful that his mom or dad had *finally* found the picture in *Field and Stream* magazine of the Zebco reel that he wanted more than anything else in the world. But most of his excitement was about the meeting tonight, where he could finally find out what was going on.

Something was wrong. Whatever it was had been brewing for two or three weeks. But Don didn't know what it was, and the not knowing gnawed at his mind like a rat chewing on a stick of wood. From the little bits of conversations he'd overheard, he *did know* it had something to do with the mine. He *did know* it had something to do with his dad. But other than that . . .

Don plopped into an empty seat near the back of the bus and slid over to the window. He glanced out to see if his little sister, Susan, was coming, then leaned back and sighed. The way he had it figured, the Christmas of 1957 was going to be the best—or worst— Christmas ever.

For two weeks, everything had been uneasy. Tense. Not an excited tense—a bad tense. It shouldn't be that way. It was Christmas— everybody ought to be a good kind of excited this time of year.

Even last night's Christmas program had felt different. The younger kids had sung "Santa Claus Is Coming to Town," just like usual. Then they sang "The First Noel," and the older kids followed that with a performance of a Christmas play.

Usually a sixth-grade boy and girl were picked to narrate, and another pair were chosen to play Mary and Joseph. A third sixth-grade boy would be the innkeeper. The rest of the fifth- and sixth-grade boys would play the wise men and the shepherds. Only this year there were only four boys in the sixth grade and ten girls. None of the boys wanted to be a narrator, so Mrs. Rayburn tried to talk Don into doing it.

He put up a fight, until . . .

Betty Martin was probably not only the smartest girl in school but also the prettiest. She had blue eyes, long blond hair, and a smile that made him feel warm all over every time he saw it.

It had been the smile that got him. That morning three weeks ago when she had stopped him in the hall and told him she was a narrator, she said she really, *really* wanted him to be the other narrator . . . well . . . he was sunk!

It was only *after* Betty Martin and Mrs. Rayburn had convinced him to take the part that he found out the principal had decided that they'd have to *memorize* their lines this year. Usually the narrators read their lines.

Things had worked out, though. Don practiced hard to learn his lines, with Mom helping him at home and Mrs. Rayburn helping him at school. And Betty and he spent a lot of time together during recess, going over their parts. The other guys had ribbed him about it, at first. Don figured it was because they were jealous. He still worried about messing up, though.

But the program went fine, and some of the guys told him it went even better than normal. And just like in years past, when the play was over, the little kids had sung "We Wish You a Merry Christmas." Finally the whole school, along with the parents, ended the program by singing "Silent Night."

Then everyone went home.

That *wasn't* normal!

There had been no standing around and visiting. No playing basketball or wrestling while the boys waited outside (for what seemed like forever), until their parents finally quit jabbering.

Everyone simply . . . went home.

A movement from the corner of Don's eye chased the curious memory away and snapped him back. Kyle slid into the seat beside him so hard and fast, Don's cheek smushed against the side of the bus.

"No sense you hogging the whole seat." Kyle jabbed him with an elbow. "Scoot over! You know I sit here."

"Can't scoot no farther," Don mumbled. "And you didn't sit here yesterday, or the day before. I figured you was mad at me or somethin'."

"I had a dentist appointment over to McAlester, remember?"

Don shrugged. "Forgot."

"Wouldn't forget if it was *you* they was workin' on." He stuck his little finger in the corner of his mouth and lifted his lip. "Two cavities. Ain't nothin' worse than hearing that drill grinding up inside your skull. Felt like that dumb old dentist was diggin' a tunnel. Trying to find a coal vein or somethin'." He slid his finger to the other side. "He just kept drilling and drilling."

Don really didn't want to look inside his friend's mouth. He gave a quick glance, then, wondering why Susan wasn't here, turned his attention back to the playground.

His baby sister stood near the jungle gym, with her fists on her hips and her chin jutting out so far a hawk could land on it. She was glaring at Amy Covington. Amy's big brother, Rex, was standing a few feet from them, grinning like an idiot—almost laughing.

Amy said something, and Susan's bottom lip quivered. Then Susan shook her head and spun toward the bus. Puffs of dust belched from beneath her shoes with each step.

Don glanced back at Kyle. His finger was out of his mouth, but Don could see the bulge in his cheek where he was feeling his new fillings with his tongue.

"What's going on around here, Kyle?" Don asked. "Nobody's excited about Christmas. People didn't hang around to visit after the program last night. Everybody seems grumpy, or mad, or crosswise with the whole world." He sighed and shook his head. "I mean . . . it don't even feel like Christmas. We've usually had a snow or two by this time of year. Hot as it's been, it feels might near like summer."

"Your dad say anything about snow?" Kyle asked.

Don shrugged. "I asked him day before

yesterday. He just shook his head. Warm as this winter's been, you reckon that might be making people uneasy?"

"Probably part of it, all right. But I think it's mostly something going on at the mine."

"What?" Don asked, almost pleading.

"How am I supposed to know? I'm just a widdle-biddy kid." Kyle stuck his thumb into his mouth like a baby. "Nobody ever tells us kids nothin'." He shook his head and made a popping sound when he pulled his thumb out. "I don't reckon there's no worse feeling than knowing something's wrong—but not knowing what. Wonder why parents do that to us?"

"Guess they don't think we'd understand." Don watched Susan get on the bus. He could almost see the tears welling up at the bottom of her eyes. "Either that or they figure it would worry us if they told what was troubling them."

When Susan finally sat down, Mrs. Sykes, the bus driver, closed the door. At last they were headed home.

"Thing is," Kyle added, "when you're

eleven, you *do* understand. And you *do* worry. Know what I mean?"

"I know." Don nodded. "Seems like you worry even more when you don't know what you're worrying about." He glanced over one shoulder, then the other, to make sure no one was listening.

"We still on for tonight?"

Kyle looked around, too. "Far as I know. But I'll call you."

"We still planning to use the fishing bit?"

Kyle nodded. "Yeah. Be careful, though. You know how Mrs. Taggert tells everything she knows."

"I know," Don assured him. "Won't breathe a word about the meeting at the town hall. Just fishing."

Whatever was bothering Susan would have to wait until they got home. Don knew good and well she wouldn't want him coming clear to the front of the bus to ask her what happened. If he brought attention to her when she was crying, or fixing to cry, she'd be mad at him for the rest of the day.

Chapter

Way I got it figured, worry is about the most stupid thing *they* do. They spend so much of their days worrying, they don't hardly have time to bury a bone or scratch a flea.

Mostly the mom and dad worry about money. Is there going to be enough to buy food? Clothes? Pay the electric bill? If they close the mine, what will happen to them? How will they live? Even if they don't close the mine, will there be enough money left over for Christmas?

When they're not worrying about money, they're worrying about the kids. Are they going to get sick? Are the kids at school going to be nice to them? Are they going to get hurt?

Sure kids are going to get sick. They come down with chicken pox, mumps, colds, earaches—all sorts of stuff. And you can bet your tail they're going to get hurt. That's just part of being a kid. Scraped knees. Scratches and falls. They can't help falling. Walking around on two legs instead of using all four—well, that's weird. Not only weird, but it takes a lot of years and a lot of practice 'fore they can keep from tipping over.

I'm there to watch, though. Got my eye on 'em. Not much can be done 'bout the little hurts, but I'm always around to make sure they don't get in too much trouble.

Still, the mom and dad worry about everything under the sun.

Don's getting just about as bad. The last few months, he's been—

A smell drifted to my nose. It broke my train of thought. I raised my head and sniffed.

Red!

Being a bloodhound I usually smell before I see. I let a minute or so go by; and when I still hadn't spotted him, I left the porch and walked to the corner of the house. Sure enough, there he was, sneaking up from the back. I knew what he was after. Don calls it stealing, but that's just 'cause he don't know the rules.

If something's lying around and ain't being

used, it's up for grabs. It's yours for the taking. 'Course, if it's yours and you ain't using it, they're welcome to get it if they want. That's just the rules.

Reckon people must have different rules.

Ducking behind the corner of the house so Red wouldn't see me, I waited until he had time to get to the big stump where I left the bone. For the life of me, I couldn't remember who had found that thing first. It was a leg bone from a cow, but there'd never been any meat on it, leastwise not since we had it. We'd been taking it back and forth between Red's house and mine for five or six months now.

Red had already started up the hill with the bone. When I was a pup, and he was still young and spry, he could usually outrun me. But he was slowing down in his old age, so I lay down beside the house and waited. When he was about halfway up the slope, I hopped up and trotted to the stump. He was watching out of the corner of one eye, so I sniffed around like I was trying to find the bone. Then I barked and chased after him.

Red was almost to the pond dam when I caught up. He lay down and put both paws on the bone.

"Mine!" he growled.

I growled back. Then we settled beside one

another and visited awhile. Later, Red got to his feet. Holding the bone high to make sure I saw it, he headed off.

In four, five days or so, I'd pay Red a visit. But as I strolled back home, I started thinking about my family again—about them worrying and being so weird. I should have asked Red if his people were being weird, too.

Last few months, Don's been worrying about being skinny. He doesn't like his bony shoulders or his knobby knees. Why a boy as tall and strong as he is would waste his time worrying about the way he looks . . . well . . . it just doesn't make sense.

He had another little worry, too—something at school last night. He had to remember a bunch of words. Not only that, but he had to stand right next to this really cute girl. Come evening, everybody would be watching. Everybody would be listening. He was worried that he might not be able to remember what he was supposed to say, or he might get the words all mixed up. Mostly he didn't want to embarrass himself in front of the pretty girl.

I guess he did fine. When they got home last night, I could feel the happy on him. I could smell how pleased he was with himself for remembering all his words. But darned if he didn't have something else worrying him. It was bothering him so bad, I couldn't even smell what it was.

Susan knows better. She plays with her doll, pets me, takes the time to smell the flowers, and laugh, and giggle. Susan doesn't waste time worrying. Susan just—

Suddenly my head snapped up. *Susan! Don!*

It was time for the bus. I raced past the old stump, around the corner of the house, up the leaning willow tree and onto the roof. When I reached the chimney, I froze. Stood perfectly still. Listened.

There was a low rumble in the distance. The sound and pitch were right. When I spotted it, my tail wagged.

The top of the big yellow school bus moved through the cedars and dogwood. I trotted down the roof and hopped the gap between the house and the shed. When all four paws were on the ground, I raced for the road.

Just as the bus's door swung open, I slid to a stop; and Don jumped from the top step. Dust puffed when he landed.

The smell on his tennis shoes made my nose

crinkle. He'd been in the bathroom, not long before he got on the bus, and one of the boys had either missed the pot or was marking his territory.

"Don," Mrs. Sykes called. "You and Susan have a merry Christmas."

"Thank you, ma'am. You too."

Susan eased down the steps. Don reached to get her elbow because the last step was pretty tall for such a little girl. Susan pulled her arm away.

"I can do it myself."

She took a deep breath. Don held his breath. I held my breath. Even Mrs. Sykes held her breath.

Susan jumped.

She landed with a thud. Her little knees almost buckled. She took a quick step, then another. Somehow she managed to catch her balance.

"Merry Christmas," she called to Mrs. Sykes.

I heard the breath *whoosh* out of the bus driver. "Merry Christmas, Susan," she called back.

Don breathed again, too.

Tail wagging with pride, I trotted over and stretched up so I could congratulate her with a kiss on the cheek.

That's when I smelled it. Sensed it.

What was this old world coming to? My ears

drooped. My tail stopped in midwag, then tucked under. *Susan was always happy. Not a care in the world. But darned if she wasn't getting as bad as the rest of the bunch. Susan was worried.*

Not just worried. She was mad, too.

Fact is, she was so mad she didn't even bother to give me a pat on the head.

Chapter

3

Don watched Susan as they walked up the drive. She didn't pay one bit of attention when ole Frank tried to give her a big lick on the cheek. She didn't pet him. Didn't even bother to shove him down or wipe the slobber off. School reader tucked under her arm, she just stomped toward the house. Judging by the amount of dust she was kicking up, Don figured she was madder than he could ever remember her.

Wonder what Amy Covington said to her? Don thought. *Whatever it was, it was bad.*

Usually he had to take short steps so Susan could keep up because his legs were a lot longer than hers. On top of that, there was usually a bunch of waiting involved. His little sister always stopped to look at a flower, or inspect a coon or coyote track in the road, or watch a bug crawl up one of the fence posts.

Today he had to stretch his long legs just to stay up with her. Instead of bouncing along ahead of them, Frank stayed behind, sniffing at her heels as if trying to figure out why she was walking so fast or what was wrong with her. Don jogged about three strides to bring himself alongside.

"Did Amy call you a bad name or something?"

Susan didn't even turn to look at him. "She's just a big, fat liar. I'm gonna tell Mama on her."

Don shrugged. *At least when we get to the house, I'll find out what's going on. Whatever it is, I bet Rex put his kid sister up to it.*

Until this year, Rex Covington had been just one of the guys. Then the Covingtons built 'em a new house. Most folks in Devlin Hollow couldn't even afford to put on a new roof, much less hire somebody to do it. But the Covingtons had a brand new house. Not as big as the Devlin Mansion, but it was still right nice and new and pretty.

At the beginning of school this year, Rex really hadn't been so bad. At least not to Don.

But when the Covingtons got their new 1958 Chevy, Rex had turned into a real snot. Fact was, if Rex didn't straighten up, one of these days Don was going to have to tear into him and—

All thoughts of Rex Covington vanished from Don's mind when Susan slammed the screen door. He barely managed to yank his hand back before the door completely smashed his fingers, but still his hand tingled. Looking down he shook it back and forth.

As he was glancing down, Frank was glancing up. Only Frank wasn't looking at him. He was staring, cross-eyed, at his nose.

"Got you, too?" Don asked. Don patted Frank on the head. Nudging the bloodhound aside with his leg, Don carefully opened the door and slipped inside.

"Mama!" Susan's plaintive cry seemed to echo through the small wood-frame house. "Mama?"

"I'm in the kitchen, dear."

Don tossed his coat onto the arm of the couch and scurried across the living room so he'd be close enough to hear what was going on. Not that he needed to be close. The way Susan was yelling, folks clear over to McAlester could probably hear her.

"Mama, Amy's mean. She's a mean, fat liar. I hate her!"

Mom shoved a pie plate into the oven, shut the door, then spun around to face Susan.

"Young lady, I don't *ever* want to hear you say that again!" she scolded. "*Hate* is a very bad word. I don't want to hear it in my house!"

Susan ducked her head. She was quiet for only a second before her head snapped up and her eyes narrowed.

"She's mean, Mama."

"What did she do, dear?"

"She lied to me. She's saying bad things to all the kids at school. She's just trying to hurt people. She makes everybody feel bad. Why does she do that, Mama?"

Mom reached out, and Susan practically flew into her arms.

Don could tell his little sister's cries. They had one sound when she was hurt—like when she fell down and scraped her knee. There was a different tone when she was mad. He'd heard that sound a time or two when she was ticked at him for something.

This time it was kind of a mix between the two. A sound Don hadn't heard and wasn't sure of. Whatever Amy Covington had done had made Susan mad—and hurt her—both at the same time.

Mom let Susan cry for a moment or two. At last she gently held Susan back at arms' length and dried the tears with her apron. Mama had the softest, most gentle hands. When Don was little, her touch always made him feel better, always helped the hurt or the mad go away.

"Did she call you a name?" Mom's voice was soft as she dabbed at the wet spots on Susan's cheeks. "Is she telling stories on you? Saying you did something you really didn't do?"

"No." Susan sniffed. "It's worse than that."

Mom's eyebrows arched. "Worse than that?"

Susan nodded.

"Did she hit you?" Don asked.

Mom shot him a look. He put his finger and thumb to his mouth, pretending to zip his lips.

Susan sniffed a couple of times. Then she took a breath.

"Amy says there ain't no Santa Claus."

"Isn't," Mom corrected.

"Amy says there *isn't* no Santa Claus. She says he ain't . . . *isn't* real. And she says that even if he is, he won't come this year 'cause Daddy wants to close the mine."

Susan started crying again. Mom hugged her close and then looked up at Don. He tried to smile at her, only it wasn't a very good smile.

Don didn't know how Mom was going to handle this one.

Chapter

ies have a smell to 'em.

Sharp as my nose was, I could pick one up from a quarter mile away. Granted I was outside, and they were inside. Still it was a warm day. Both front and back doors were open. The screens let the air flow through the house.

When Mom started talking, I sniffed.

"Honey, there are lots of folks who don't believe in Santa Claus. There are lots of folks who do. And I reckon the folks who don't believe figure they're smarter than the rest of us. I reckon they think they know something that we don't; and they got to take it on themselves to try and tell the whole world that they're right, and everybody else is wrong."

"But Amy says that the reason nobody ever sees him is because he ain . . . *isn't* . . . real. He's just made up. Have *you* ever seen Santa Claus, Mama?"

"I've never seen the ocean, Susan, but I know it's there. Your dad told me all about it when he came back from the war. I've never seen the wind, but I can see what it does. And I've never seen Santa Claus."

Susan leaned forward, looking Mom straight in the eye.

"Are you and Daddy Santa Claus?"

Mom kind of tilted her head to one side, like she was thinking. Then she nodded. I couldn't smell a lie.

"I reckon we are," she smiled. "I reckon you and Don are, too."

Susan blinked.

"Remember when we went to McAlester last Christmas for that big parade?" Mom asked. "You asked Daddy if that was the *real* Santa Claus on the float. What did he say?"

Susan nibbled at her bottom lip, thinking on it for a spell.

"Daddy said that wasn't the real Santa. He was just one of his helpers."

"And remember picking those tennis shoes out

for Don last year? That made you one of Santa's helpers, too, didn't it?"

Still nibbling her bottom lip, Susan shrugged. "I guess."

Mom nodded. "Santa's got lots of helpers. And I'm like you; I've never seen him. What I *have* seen—ever since I was a little girl—is people being nice to one another this time of year. People who usually walk around with frowns on their faces, all of a sudden smiling and saying howdy. People suddenly becoming quiet and polite and respectful. Like at the end of the Christmas program last night, when you first- and second-graders started 'Silent Night.' The whole town joined in. I felt the chills race up my arms and my back.

"Maybe what we call Santa Claus is just a feeling—a spirit or something—that kinda sneaks up and grabs hold of people's hearts around Christmastime. I reckon he makes people think about Jesus and what a wonderful gift God gave this old world. Maybe for no more than a moment or two, lets them know . . . no, remember . . . what Christmas is really about. To me that's about as *real* as it gets. What do you think?"

There was still no lie smell. But when Mom

asked Susan, "What do you think?" my tail stopped in midswing. I watched Susan. Waited. Finally a smile lifted the corners of her mouth.

"I think Santa Claus is real."

When she said it, all the mad and hurt and worry were gone from her. Susan was back to being Susan again. My tail thumped so hard it almost broke.

"I don't care what Amy says. I believe he's real," Susan said.

With that she gave Mom a big hug and a kiss. Then she turned to Don, squeezed him really hard, and skipped off to her room.

Don shot Mom a quick glance and then turned to watch Susan.

"Hey, brat," he called. "What do you want Santa to bring you for Christmas?"

Susan paused at the door of her room for only a second.

"Santa knows."

Don turned to Mom and raised his eyebrows. She shrugged.

"Do *you* know what she wants?" he whispered.

"Not a clue."

About then the phone rang.

"That might be Kyle," Don said. "We heard the catfish were biting at the lake this week. Since there's no school tomorrow, you think it'd be all right if we get in some fishing this evening?"

"Can I go, too?" Susan called from her room.

"No!"

The look on Mom's face, when he roared at Susan, made Don flinch. The phone rang a second time. Mom sighed and shook her head. "We'll see."

Suddenly the smell hit me. All the time Mom was talking, I couldn't smell a thing. But with those few words from Don about fishing—the way his fingers tensed and relaxed at his side . . . well . . .

Like I said, lies have a smell to them. What I smelled was a downright *stink.*

Chapter
5

Don said thank you when Mom handed him the phone. He held the receiver to his ear, and hesitated a second, until she walked out of the kitchen.

"Hello, Kyle?" he whispered.

The phone crackled, but Kyle didn't answer.

"Kyle? Are you there?"

Nothing but a dull, hollow, crackling hum came from the phone. Then, "Alice?" Mrs. Taggert asked. "Are you there?"

Don pulled the phone from his ear for only an instant and frowned.

"No. This is Don."

"Don. Mrs. Taggert. Leslie Sparks needed to speak with Kyle's mother while I was waiting for you to pick up. Just stay on the line. Soon as she's through visiting, I'll ring Kyle back. Okay?"

"Yes, ma'am. Thank you, Mrs. Taggert."

Don sat with the phone to his ear, listening to the dull empty hum. While he waited, he couldn't help but think that Devlin Hollow had to be the most backward town in the whole country.

Last summer they'd driven up to Kansas City to visit Uncle George. He and Aunt Beverly had *dial* telephones—two of 'em. All you had to do was stick your finger in the holes and spin the dial around to the numbers you wanted. When Mom's sister, Elizabeth, had her first baby, they drove to Birmingham to see her. Same thing. Seemed like the whole world, except for Devlin Hollow, had those newfangled, modern—

"Don?" Mrs. Taggert's voice made him jerk. "I'm ringing Kyle for you now."

"Thank you."

He could hear the phone ringing, but Mrs. Benson picked it up instead of Kyle. "Hang on a second, Don. I'll get him for you," she said.

"Don?"

"Kyle?" Don asked back; then quickly, knowing Mrs. Taggert was probably still on the line, added: "You find out if you could go *fishing* this evening?" He stressed the word *fishing* so Kyle would know Mrs. Taggert was still listening.

"Ah . . ." Kyle hesitated. "Mama said it was okay. What did your mom say?"

"I asked her, but we kind of got interrupted. I think it'll be okay, though."

There was a long silence. Both boys waited, listening and trying to determine if the telephone operator was still eavesdropping.

It was common knowledge around Devlin Hollow that Molly Taggert could stay on the line without making a sound for an entire conversation. Dale McMullan, who had the fastest hot rod in the whole county, had said that there was no way Sheriff Whitener and four highway-patrol cars could have been waiting at Baker's Flats, if Mrs. Taggert hadn't told him about the big four-county drag race last spring.

Poor Dale had spent the last five months of his senior year walking every place he went. And when he graduated from high school, his parents sold his 1956 Chevy Bel Air with the turbo 350 V8 engine and dual carbs, and bought him what he called a "puke green" Studebaker.

'Course the way Don figured it, the big drag race wasn't all that much of a secret. Last year he was in fifth grade, and all the kids in his class knew about it at least two weeks before-hand. Maybe Mrs. Taggert *wasn't* to blame. Seeing as how practically everybody in four counties knew about the big drag race, there were lots of people who could have let it slip. But it could have been Molly Taggert.

"You still there, Don?"

"Yeah."

"I hear that the catfish start hitting around seven. Might ought to get to the lake about six or six-fifteen, so as we can get all our gear set up."

That meant Kyle had found out when the meeting started.

"Sounds good to me," Don answered to let Kyle know he understood. "You sure that'll give us enough time to . . . uh . . . set up."

"Sure. I'll bring some of Dad's stink-bait and dough bait. That five-pound coffee can you got still have worms in it?"

"Haven't checked them in a while, but I think they're all right. Where . . . uh . . . are the catfish feeding? Up by the dam?"

There was a pause. "Yeah. I . . . uh . . . I think that would be the best place. Yeah. West side."

"See ya there around six. Bye."

"Don." Kyle stopped him. "If you find out you aren't gonna be able to make it, give me a call 'fore I leave the house, okay?"

"Right. See ya in a little bit."

There was a distinct click when Kyle hung up the phone. Holding his breath, Don hesitated. There was nothing but silence through the receiver. He held his breath so long, he was afraid he might pop. An instant before he had to let it out, the silence was replaced by the dull, crackling, hollow hum.

With a smile, Don let the air whish from his lungs. *Caught you*, he thought with a smile. *Dale McMullen was right all along. It probably was Molly Taggert who ratted on him.*

Don went to his room and dug around at the back of his closet until he came up with the old shoes he used for mowing the lawn and fishing. They were a size or so too small, and the little toe on his left foot sometimes poked through the seam between the side and the rubber soles. It didn't matter. If he tried to leave the house to go "fishing" in his school clothes or good shoes, Mom was bound to get suspicious.

He found an old sweatshirt that had oil stains on the front and the jeans he wore when the guys got together for football. Once dressed he paused in front of his dresser mirror for an instant and grinned at the reflection. *Looks like a fisherman to me.*

Mom pulled the chicken out of the oven, used her hot-pad to lift the roaster lid, and peeked inside.

"Is it about ready?" Don asked.

She glanced over her shoulder at him. "Almost. Could you fetch me a jar of green beans from the cellar?"

"Yes, ma'am. Reckon Dad wants to go fishin' with me?" he asked, pausing at the back screen.

"Doubt it. There's a meeting at the town hall tonight. Figure he's going to that."

Don started to shove the screen open, then paused again. "Why are they having a meeting? What are they gonna talk about?"

Mom slid the roasting pan back in the oven. She turned toward him—but only part way—then turned back to close the oven door. "It's . . . just something about the mine."

Didn't think she'd give me a straight answer, Don grumped to himself. *Least she didn't say no to the fishing. Kyle and I will just find out for ourselves what's going on.*

Dad was washing up by the old pump when Don walked out the back door. Frank lay beside him, watching. Dad always washed the coal dust off himself before he came inside.

"Hi, Dad. Everything go okay at the mine today?"

"Hi, Don," his dad said, pulling his shirt off to shake some of the dust out. "Everything went well as could be expected. How was school?"

"Well as could be expected," he answered, giving his dad as much information as Dad had given him. "Least we don't have to go back for two weeks."

Working the pump handle with his right hand, Dad stuck his head under the spigot. Don waited. When Dad came up for air, he took the towel from the hook beside the wash-basin table. "Ask your mom to put a bucket of water on the stove for me," he said, after drying his hair for a moment or two. "There's a meeting tonight. Might as well go ahead and get my bath."

"Got to fetch her a jar of green beans first," Don said. "I'll tell her when I take the beans in."

To Don it seemed like it took forever to eat. He was ready to go meet Kyle at the dam, put their fishing stuff where nobody would find it, then get to town. They'd find a good place to hide and watch until all the men were inside the meeting hall. Then . . . at last . . . maybe he could find out what was going on and why people were acting so strange.

Wait until everyone finished eating; wait for Dad to take his bath . . . wait, wait, wait. It was almost as bad as waiting for the bell to ring on the last day of school before Christmas vacation.

Chapter

Okay! Things were smelling stinky again.

Hedging or skirting around the truth has a smell to it. It don't stink as bad as an out-and-out lie. It do smell though. Worry? That's a totally different odor. But for a bloodhound . . . we can sniff out each separate one of them, clear as a fresh raccoon trail.

I could smell what was going on even from out on the back porch. When they let me inside for supper, I was right in the middle of things. 'Course, the chicken scraps and biscuits Mom added to my bowl distracted me for a minute or two. When she cooked homemade biscuits, she always made four extra for me. Biscuits, chicken scraps, and gravy sure made the dog food taste downright larrupin'.

After I finished eating, I could tell there was a lot more going on at the meeting hall than "just something about the mine." Mom knew *that* as well as Dad did. They were just shading the truth by not talking about it in front of the kids. It didn't smell like an out-and-out lie. They were worried, too. Mom was worried about Dad. Dad was worried about his friends, the men he worked with. And like always, they were both worried about money and Christmas and their kids. Don was worried about Mom and Dad. He was also worried about getting caught. Why he was worried about getting caught, I had no idea. It usually meant he'd done something he wasn't supposed to do, or he was going to do something. And . . . sprinkled in with all those aromas was a hint of worry about what Susan wanted for Christmas.

My nose was popping, working really hard to sort out all the different feelings. Then right before Dad left, he smeared some of that stinky stuff under his armpits. You talk about a gosh-awful smell. It was enough to make my eyes water.

Dad thought it made him smell good. About the only time he used it was when they were headed to Sunday church or to a wedding or something. But the stuff was awful. I mean, if he really wanted to smell good—if he really wanted to impress someone—why didn't he just roll in something dead? Talk about a wonderful fragrance. It's enough to make the old heart palpitate. And the girls . . . when they get a whiff of . . . well . . . anyway, the stuff Dad put on messed up my sniffer for a good twenty minutes or so.

About the time it cleared, Don went to the shed to get his coffee can full of worms and his fishing rods. He had his weights and fishhooks in a tin bucket that was big enough to set the worm can inside. Carrying the bucket and worms in one hand and his two rods in the other, he stepped to the back porch. Mom and Susan were finishing up the dishes.

"Going to meet Kyle at the lake," he called.

Mom glanced over her shoulder. "You two boys stay out of the water. I know it's been warm for a couple of weeks, but that lake is cold as ice. You understand?"

"Yes, ma'am."

"When do you think you'll be back?"

"If the fish are bitin', we should be able to catch a mess in an hour or two. If not, we might try staying awhile longer. I'm not sure."

That lie stunk! Major stink!

"Be careful."

"Yes, ma'am."

There was no doubt in my mind that Don was up to something! I shoved the screen open with my nose. No way was I gonna let this kid out of my sight. Whatever it was that he was about to do, it was something he wasn't supposed to. Like I said, you can't keep kids from getting hurt—scrapes, banged up knees, scratches. But when they're into something serious—something they know good and well they're not supposed to do—they might need help.

The lake was less than a mile from our house. Each morning Dad walked to the west side of the dam, crossed over, and went another half mile up on the ridge to the mine entrance. Staying ahead of Don, I led the way, following Dad's trail as we went.

At the dam, Don stopped. So did I. Another sniff told me Dad's trail went off to the left this time—he wasn't going to the mine. Devlin Hollow was down the hill. Must be headed there.

The breeze drifted up the valley from all the houses. People smells, different things they cooked for supper, cars . . . all sorts of stuff. I guess that's why my ears picked up the sound before my nose knew someone was coming. A shape was moving toward us from the other side of the dam. I stuck my nose in the air and flared my nostrils.

Kyle.

I barked and wagged my tail, so Don would know we had company. He finally looked around and waved, but Kyle didn't wave back. He was carrying too much fishing gear. Don waited until Kyle got to him; then they walked down to the lake. But just like I suspected, they didn't bait their hooks or throw their lines into the water. Instead they put all their gear between two fallen oak logs.

Glancing about to make sure the gear was hidden from view, they quickly climbed back to the edge of the dam. I picked up Dad's trail again. They followed. But when we got to town, they veered off the path and took one of the side streets. Not quite sure where we were going, I left the scent to stay with them.

Kyle and Don moved like two snails crawling up a wall—cautious, sneaky, from one tree to the next. When we reached the road where the town hall was, they peered around the corner of Andrew Bleu's General Store.

From there on, it was like watching a couple of cats sneaking up on a bird. Almost tiptoeing, they crossed the street very slowly. A group of boys were already standing at the back windows of the town hall, peeking in. Don and Kyle must have figured it was too crowded to go there. They crept down the sidewalk until they got to the first open window.

Bad smells came from that window—so many of the bad feelings that people have, all rolled together—and so thick they almost clogged my nose. There was anger, fear, envy, jealousy, distrust, even a couple of odors I didn't recognize. The mean voices that came from inside made the little tingly hairs on my back stand up in a ridge, from my ears down to the tip of my tail.

A little quiver ran through me when I heard Dad's voice boom above all the rest.

Chapter

7

Don watched as his father stood in the midst of all the shaking fists, pointing fingers, and angry voices. Dad held up his hands, asking them to be quiet. Slowly at first, the men looked at him, then began to sit down. There were still more shouts and sharp words. But after a moment or two, Dad was the only one left standing, and the angry noise settled to a low rumble.

Dad cleared his throat. "Hans, Paul didn't say he was planning to fire anybody. And Paul, no one in here has even mentioned the word *strike*. This isn't about more pay or better working conditions."

There was a platform at the front of the room, a podium, and a table with two chairs. An old guy named Connor Leverett sat in one. Paul Covington stood behind the wooden podium, shaking his finger at the crowd and at Dad.

"Then what *is* it about, Delbert?" Paul snapped. "You guys want to keep half the mine closed. If that ain't a *strike*, then what do you call it?"

Again people sprang to their feet, yelling things like:

"Crook!"

"Liar!"

"Mine-owner stooge!"

Others shouted at Dad with words that made Don's blood boil:

"Troublemaker!"

"You're the reason they closed that side of the mine in the first place!"

"Coward!"

Don felt his fists clench at his sides. Dad just stood there until others quieted their furious coworkers.

When the noise faded, he cleared his throat. "We called for an inspection. The Bureau of Mines ordered the east shafts closed, and some of the men—"

"Yeah," somebody called, "that's only because *you* voted to have them come in."

Dad waited for the noise to settle. "Some of the men"—he repeated—"good men who have been mining all their lives feel that the Bureau of Mines should decide whether it's safe to go back in again. That's all we're asking."

"Our engineer already checked it! Just two weeks ago!" Paul shouted. "He said it was fine. No danger at all."

"Gordon Bell works for the owners. Not for us!" someone yelled from the crowd. "He'd tell us breathing methane gas was good for us, if that's what the owners told him to say."

The angry roar that followed was as loud and quick as a clap of thunder. Men sprang to their feet. Shouted. Cursed.

As far as Don could see, the only ones who weren't involved in the shouting were his dad and Connor Leverett. Mr. Leverett was an old man with white hair—probably the oldest guy in the room and one of the oldest miners. He rested his elbows on the table. Calm and relaxed, he watched the commotion for a while. Finally he eased from his chair and stepped to the podium.

His broad shoulders and big, calloused rough hands belied his frail, drawn face and spindly legs. He tried to nudge Paul Covington aside. When Paul didn't budge, he nudged a little harder, sending Paul staggering, almost off the edge of the platform. Paul glared at him.

Mr. Leverett ignored the angry stare and rapped on the podium with his knuckles. When that didn't work, he slapped the wood with his open hand, so hard and sharp it sounded like gunfire. Almost everybody stopped to see what was going on.

"Thank you, gentlemen." He spoke so softly, the men had to be even quieter to hear. "As duly elected parliamentarian of this fine organization, I'm now taking charge of this here meetin'. There are two reasons for this. The first is in that book over yonder," he said, pointing at the table where he'd been sitting. "The *Parliamentary Procedure Manual* says that folks got to be recognized by the chairman before they can start shootin' their mouths off. You gentlemen ain't doing that. You're acting like a bunch of rowdy schoolboys, trying to pick a fight on the playground.

"The second reason I'm taking charge is 'cause my daughter and her family drove in from Chicago yesterday. I got two grandsons to play with, instead of wasting my whole night here!

"Now *every single one of you* sit down and shut up!" He glanced over his shoulder. "That means you too, Paul."

"But I'm the president," he protested.

Mr. Leverett smiled and nodded his head. "I know that. I'm one of the guys who voted for you. Now . . . sit down in your chair over yonder and shut . . . up!"

Paul stomped grudgingly behind him and plopped into the other folding chair at the table. Mr. Leverett grabbed hold of both sides of the podium and leaned forward.

"From now on, if you got something to say, raise your hand. *If* I call your name, you can stand up, say your piece, then sit back down. Ain't nobody else gonna talk! *Everybody got that?* When one guy's done, someone else can raise a hand; and *if* I call his name, he can stand up and say his piece.

"You hooligans don't do this, I'm gonna end the meeting until everybody cools down. That means the owners won't get any coal mined. They'll lose money. And you miners ain't getting paid, 'cause you're not working. You're sittin' in here, griping at one another. Everybody loses.

"Now . . . anybody got a question?"

The men shook their heads and stayed quiet—all except one of the younger miners. He bounced up and down in his chair, flopping his hand around in the air like he was fighting a bumblebee.

"Ron Callison," Mr. Leverett called. "You got a question?"

The young man nodded and stood. "Can you do that? I mean, make us come back tomorrow for a meeting instead of going to work?"

"I just did." Mr. Leverett grinned. "Now if you don't think I *can*, I'll lend you that book over yonder; and you can take it home and read it for yourself—*after* the meeting!"

The young man glanced at the thick book on the table and sank back into his chair.

"Anybody else?"

When no one raised a hand, he pointed at Dad. "Delbert Franklin. You were the last one talking when all this got started. You have the floor."

Dad cleared his throat. "The Bureau of Mines closed the east shafts. They're the ones who should inspect the repairs and tell us if it's safe to reopen them."

Some of the men applauded.

"Knock it off," Mr. Leverett growled. He turned to the table beside him.

"Paul Covington. You're next. After him the rest of you need to raise your hands and wait till I call your name 'fore you say *one single word*."

Paul stood and started toward the podium. Mr. Leverett nodded at his chair.

"They can hear you just fine from there, Paul. And keep it short. No long-winded speeches."

Paul sneered at him and then turned to the group.

"Moving everyone to the west shafts made them crowded, and our coal production is down. The owners have added timbers in the east shafts. The engineer says it's safe. I say it's safe. If we don't open up the whole mine soon, they might close it down altogether. We don't need a bunch of 'outsiders' telling us our business." He paused a moment. "The only problem we have here is that Delbert Franklin and two or three of his buddies are afraid to go down in the earth and dig. Three or four *scared* men are messing up the whole works for the rest of us."

Kyle nudged Don. "I can't believe he said that!"

Don didn't say anything. He was shaking so hard he couldn't talk. Paul was calling his dad a coward. For the life of him, he couldn't understand how his father could sit there so calm and not jump up and punch Paul right in the nose.

"Keith Benson," Mr. Leverett called. When he said Kyle's dad's name, both boys turned their attention back to the meeting hall.

"Yes, sir," Mr. Benson began. "Reckon lots of folks are worried about their jobs, especially here at Christmastime. And I figure a whole bunch of you forgot that when we voted to have the Bureau of Mines come and check the east shafts, we had a tie vote. For some of you who might have forgot what a tie vote is . . . that means *half* the people in here—not just a few men, but *half*—voted to call for a safety inspection of the mine. Since Mr. Covington was away on business, and since Mr. Leverett was home with the flu, and since Delbert was vice president, he *had to vote* to break the tie. To me half the miners sounds like a little bigger number than two or three."

Mr. Benson paused a moment and looked around at the men. Then he smiled. "It also seems to me like Mr. Covington is more interested in keeping his cushy job than he is in the safety of the men he works with. Paul's the coward, not Delbert."

Instantly an uproar started; and almost as quickly, Mr. Leverett pounded the podium.

"Quiet!!!"

"Whether you like Paul Covington or Delbert Franklin," Mr. Leverett roared, "it don't matter. Stick to what we're talking about. Kendall Washington. Your turn."

The men took turns. Most of the worry seemed to be about what they would do if the mine owners closed the mine. Others said that underground mining was almost dead in Oklahoma, and most digs had already turned to strip-mining. The big concern was being out of work—especially at Christmas.

The debate seemed to go on forever, until Mark O'Ryan stood up. He was as old as Mr. Leverett—maybe even older. "The reason we took the vote in the first place was that more than one of the miners heard timbers cracking. Mr. Leverett wasn't the only one sick with the flu that night. I was, too. Had both of us been here, there wouldn't have been a tie." He paused a moment, giving everyone time to see Connor Leverett nodding his head.

"First year Connor and me went down in the earth to dig coal," Mr. O'Ryan continued, "we were both just kids. Reckon fourteen or fifteen—so long ago that I don't rightly remember. But . . . both of us were at Adamson Number One."

A sudden silence swept through the crowd. It was so quiet that it sent a chill scampering up the back of Don's neck. It was the first time the whole room had been *totally* still since he and Kyle got there.

Mr. O'Ryan wiped a hand across his mouth. "Reckon this fuss is about money—losing our jobs. We're trying to find someone to blame. I'll tell you this straight up. I won't go into the east shafts until they've been inspected by the Bureau of Mines."

When Rendz Jovonovich stood up to say his piece, Don didn't hear what he said. That's because somebody shoved him away from the window.

He looked around. Rex Covington was there. Two older boys, Lloyd Koehler and Billy Walsh, stood on either side.

"Your dad's a coward!" Rex shouted.

Lloyd pushed Kyle against the wall. "And your dad's a filthy liar."

Chapter

8

Short of biting one of them on the leg, there wasn't a darned thing I could do. The fight happened so fast I didn't even have time to get between Don and Rex to try and keep them apart.

When all was said and done, Kyle had a torn shirt and a busted lip. Don had a puffy eye. Rex's nose was bleeding like mad. Lloyd had a lump on the side of his head that made one ear stick out farther than the other. One boy, who I didn't even know, got bit—not by me—by one of the other boys.

When all the pushing, shoving, yelling, and swinging started, a whole herd of boys jumped in.

My paws were sore from getting stepped on, and my tail got crunched so hard it's a wonder it didn't break. What started out with five boys, turned into nine or twelve.

It's a wonder I got off as easy as I did.

All the commotion brought the men streaming out of the meeting hall to break up the fighting. Then each boy's father came outside to take care of his own. By the time Dad got through with Don and sent him on his way, the walk home was downright gloomy. If Don had a tail, it would have been tucked so far under his belly that the tip would have been flipping him on the nose.

Neither boy said a word until we got to where they had hidden their fishing gear. Instead of picking up his things, Kyle plopped down on one of the logs.

"Reckon I'm gonna get a bustin' over this deal."

Don nodded. "Me too."

"My dad uses a coal scoop he keeps near the potbellied stove. What does your dad use?"

"Hickory switch. He claims it's the same one his dad used on him. Says he brought it along from Pennsylvania when they moved here."

"Ever switched you with it?"

Don nodded his head. "Only once, though. I was about six or seven. I don't remember for sure, but we were at a store somewhere in McAlester. A Ben Franklin store, I think. I found this toy I wanted; and when Mom said no, I threw a fit. Must have been a good one, too. Dad didn't say a word. He just snatched me up, and both of us went to the car— me squalling and him just sitting—until Mom got finished with her shopping. But when we got home . . ."

I saw Don's hair flip when he shot a blast of air up his forehead.

Kyle got to his feet. He stood there a long time, just looking down at his fishing stuff. Finally he let out a long sigh. "Shoulda gone fishin'."

Don just nodded. "Shoulda."

I followed at Don's heels while he put his fishing things in the shed. Mom was sitting on the couch, darning one of Dad's work socks. Susan was curled in a ball, sleeping next to her. Don held the door and let me come inside.

"You're home early." Mom smiled. "Guess the fish were really biting."

Don stood there, head hung low and hands fidgeting at his sides. He didn't look at her. Fact was he kind of stood sideways, trying to keep his left eye so she couldn't see it.

"We didn't go fishing," he confessed, his

voice soft so as not to wake Susan. "Kyle and me snuck down to the meeting hall."

My tail froze in midswing. I flattened my ears, expecting the noise to be pretty loud when she got onto him.

Instead of yelling, Mom just started running the needle and thread through the sock she was working on. "Figured as much."

"You learn anything?" she asked, still concentrating on the sock.

"Like what's going on at the mine?"

"No. Like when to duck if somebody throws a punch."

Don shuffled from one foot to the other, looking around.

"I–I guess . . . I shoulda ducked," he stammered. "Either that or put my hands up. Only I didn't have any idea Rex was gonna hit me."

Mom stuck her sewing needle into the arm of the couch and laid the sock beside it. "Got a piece of round steak in the icebox. Come on."

I followed them and crawled under the table.

She handed him the piece of meat and motioned to the table. "Hold that on your eye for a while. It'll help the swelling go down."

When Mom told Don it was time for bed, they put me outside. I stayed on the porch until Dad got home. Sniffed him up good when he stopped to pet me before he opened the front door.

There was still a smell of worry on him, but no angry or mad. Even so, as soon as he shut the door, I raced around the corner of the house to stand outside Don's bedroom. When Dad didn't come in to switch Don, I curled up, licked my sore paws, and finally fell asleep.

Chapter
9

"Morning, sleepyhead," Mom greeted Don when he shuffled into the kitchen for breakfast. "How's the eye?"

"It's fine," Don answered. "It don't even hurt no more."

"Anymore," Mom corrected.

"Anymore. Where's Dad?"

"Getting ready for work. He didn't come home till one this morning. I let him sleep a few extra minutes."

Don staggered across the kitchen and sat at his place. Susan was already digging into her cereal.

"Got biscuits with sausage 'n' gravy. Or you can have cereal with your sister."

"Biscuits 'n' gravy." Don yawned. "Is Dad mad at me?"

When Mom didn't answer, Don suddenly felt more awake. He didn't get a chance to ask again. Dad walked in, poured himself a cup of coffee, and sat down across the table.

"Sure smells good, Alice. How are you this morning, Susan?"

When she looked up to grin at her dad, a little milk dribbled from the corner of her mouth.

Then Dad looked at Don. Don shifted nervously from one cheek to the other when Dad stared at him. But he didn't say anything. After a second or two, Dad looked down into his coffee cup and took a sip. "Coffee's right good, too."

Don felt one of his knees bouncing underneath the table. His left hand shook. Finally realizing he couldn't take the silence or the suspense any longer, he blurted out, "Are you gonna switch me, Dad?"

Dad took the coffee cup from his lips. He didn't look up, but just stared down into the cup.

"Maybe later."

Don was shaking and wiggling so much, he could almost hear the chair rattling beneath him. When Mom set his biscuits and gravy on the table in front of him, he couldn't even reach for it. He was trembling so hard, the gravy would have gone flying all over the place. He wanted to jump up and run. Either that or race to the washroom, grab the hickory switch, and tell Dad to "get it over with." It felt as if he sat there for an eternity before Dad finally looked up from his coffee cup.

Smiled.

"Not gonna switch you . . . *this* time." Dad set his cup down. "Don't hold with fighting. You know that. But Connor Leverett pointed out that we were acting like a bunch of hooligans, and we shouldn't expect our sons to act more grown up than we were.

"Don't hold with lying to your mom, neither." He took another sip of his coffee. "But we talked it over last night, and . . . well . . . the reason we didn't say much about what was going on at the mine . . . it's Christmastime. We didn't want to worry you kids. But the way everybody's been acting lately, we should have figured you knew something was wrong. Guess if we'd been more open and honest with you, you would have been more honest with us. But . . ."

He set his coffee cup down again, propped one elbow on the table, and shook his finger so close to Don's nose that Don had to look cross-eyed to focus on it.

". . . but," he repeated, "if it ever happens again, we ain't making any excuses for you. And any excuses you come up with for fighting or lying ain't gonna hold water. I'll bust you so hard, you won't be able to sit down for a week. Got me?"

"Yes sir."

Mom brought Dad his plate, and they settled down to breakfast. 'Course, about the time they got settled, Susan was finished with her cereal. She asked if she could take Frank outside to play. Mom glanced at his food bowl. Don did, too. Old Frank's bowl was licked clean as a whistle. He sat there, watching the table to see if anyone dropped something that he could swoop in on and clean up. When he saw them looking at him, Don could hear Frank's tail thumping on the floor. Mom nodded. "Stay close to the house. This is laundry day."

Susan was gone in a flash.

By the time they finished breakfast, Don

had calmed himself down. He got his nerve together enough to ask something that had been bothering him since the meeting last night.

"Dad?"

"Yes, Don?"

"What's the Adamson Number One mine? And why did all the guys get so quiet when Mr. O'Ryan said he was there?"

Mom and Dad fell silent. Dad put his fork down and shoved his plate aside. He picked up his coffee cup, but he didn't drink.

"Adamson was the name of a town here in Oklahoma," he began, his voice so soft that Don felt chills. "It was on the other side of McAlester from us and reckon it was about the same size as Devlin Hollow. Maybe a little bigger. It was named for the mine owner, Peter Adamson. I don't know if he owned any more mines, but Adamson Number One is what people remember.

"Back in 1914, about the middle of August, a miner by the name of Levine was down in one of the shafts and heard a timber cracking. They sounded the horns and cleared the mine. The next day, the engineer, owner, and four miners went down to check things out. They found that the supports were fine and there was no problem, so they opened the mine again.

"Early to mid-September, Levine and one of the other miners told his foreman that they heard a timber crack. They sounded the alarm again. Word or gossip has it that folks didn't seem in too much of a rush. Not until—"

He broke off to take a sip of his coffee. "Most of the miners either walked or ran out. Ones from the lower levels rode the trips. By the time most were coming out, everybody could hear the cracking. Men still in the tunnels said they heard splintering supports from below. Reckon it was 'cause the tunnels and rooms of the mine squeezed and started to collapse. Most made it out. Up top they say it sounded like an explosion. The whole mine collapsed within a matter of minutes. The mountain itself sank. Dropped about ten to twelve feet."

Don felt ten times tighter and tense, listening to Dad's story, than he had when he was worrying about a switching. He swallowed the thickness in his throat.

"Dad? You said *most* of the men . . ."

Still staring into his coffee cup, Dad nodded.

"There were thirteen miners working the very bottom room of the mine. Levine went back after them. Everybody made it out except for those fourteen. When the whole mine collapsed, there was no way they could rescue anybody. There wasn't even any chance of recovering the bodies."

With a sigh, he glanced up at the clock above the kitchen stove.

"Well . . . time to get to work. See ya later."

He ruffled Don's hair. Mom looked up from the dishes long enough to kiss him on the cheek. Then he was out the back door.

When the back screen bounced shut, Don sat there for only an instant. He sprang to his feet and started after his dad. A plate crashed to the floor when Mom spun to catch him by the arm.

"I don't want him to go," he said, fighting as hard as he could to say the words instead of screaming them. "I don't want Dad to—"

"Stop, Don! Keep your voice down." Her

tone was quiet yet stern. "Come sit with me at the table." Once there she patted his arm. "Your dad is a miner. He goes down in the earth to work, to make a living."

"But, Mom . . ."

"There's no 'buts.' That's just the way it is."

"But . . ."

"He's going to be fine. After things settled down last night, they decided to call the Bureau of Mines and have someone come to reinspect the tunnels. In the meantime, they took a vote to see if they would stay out of the east shafts. It was so close they couldn't decide. So each crew took a vote as to whether they would go down. When that turned out mixed, one of the men suggested that they divide up. The ones who were convinced that it *wasn't* safe could, temporarily, work with foremen on the west shafts. Men who thought it *was* safe could go with the foremen and crews who wanted to start back on the east. Your dad's a foreman. He and his crew will be digging coal in the west shafts. The east shafts are probably safe; but whether they are or not, your dad will *not* be there. He and his crew will be doing just what they've done for the past six months."

Don felt a little better. But remembering Dad's face . . . remembering the strange tone of his voice . . . when he told about the Adamson mine . . . the fear grabbed hold of him again. He felt like every muscle was tight as a stretched rubber band.

"Then why did Dad still seem so scared and upset? I could see it, Mom," he tried to explain. "I could see it in his eyes. I could hear it in his voice."

Mom patted his hand.

"Your dad wasn't scared for himself. He was scared for the other men. They're miners, Don. They're like family. And like families, they don't always agree. They argue, and fuss, and . . . sometimes . . . yes, they even fight. But that doesn't mean they don't love one another. It doesn't mean they don't care.

"Your dad doesn't want anybody to get hurt. And . . . hard as it is for you to under-stand . . . Paul Covington feels the same. If something happened to your dad or his crew, Paul and his men would be the first ones back down in the mine. They wouldn't worry whether it was safe or not. They wouldn't think about another cave-in. They'd run over one another, trying to get down there so they could rescue their friends."

She gave his hand a gentle squeeze, then eased from her chair to go pick up the broken pieces of the plate she had dropped. Don stood there a moment, watching her.

"Is it *really* safe? I mean . . . you know . . . being stuck underground and digging for coal?"

Mom didn't look up. "Safe as anything else. You get right down to it, walking to town can be dangerous. Especially with all the cars people are running around in nowadays. Why don't you go out and play with Susan and Frank? Try not to think about it. Think about something else." She put the pieces of the broken plate in the trash, then turned and popped her dish towel at him. "I know what will keep your mind busy. See if you can think of a way to get Susan to tell you what she wants for Christmas. Your dad and I haven't been able to get a thing out of her, and we're running out of time."

Chapter

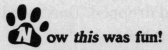 ow *this* was fun!

Susan found the rubber ball they got for me three years ago. It had a little jingly thing inside. The first one I'd ever had was just like it. I'd been bound and determined to find out what was making that noise, I gnawed and pawed and chewed till I finally got the little silver thing out. Only problem: It didn't jingle no more.

Seeing's how I kind of liked the little noise it made, I just chewed on this one instead of trying to dig for the jingly thing. Susan threw it. I fetched it. Over and over and over again.

The four biscuits and sausage gravy Mom put on my dog food were scrumptious. Only after chasing that ball fifteen or so times, for some strange reason, my tummy didn't feel good.

I ran after the ball one last time; but instead of

fetching it, I took it around the corner of the house, dropped it in the weeds beside the shed, and ate some grass. That settled my stomach. Susan hunted for the ball but not very long. She found some raccoon tracks and tried to follow them.

Don joined us about thirty yards up the ridge. He was as tense as one of the strings on Dad's banjo. That's people for you. Worry. Worry. Worry.

But this time the feel and smell I got from him was different. Don wasn't worried about being too skinny. He didn't care if his knees were knobby or if his shoulders were too bony. He wasn't concerned about being next to a pretty girl while everybody in town watched him. He didn't care that he might forget what he was supposed to say.

Don was worried about his dad. Mom told him Dad was okay. When Dad left for the mine, he felt happy. Mostly because he had done what he knew was right. But still Don was worried.

To make it even worse, he was trying hard not to pass it to Susan.

Well, I guess people are like that. Guess if they ain't got something to worry about, they just have to go find something.

Sounding *too* bright and cheerful, Don asked Susan what she was looking at. When she pointed at animal tracks, he helped her find another, then another. A ways up the hill, where the tracks ran out, they found a pack-rat nest in a crevice between some rocks. Using a stick to scrape the twigs aside, they explored it.

"Don't tell me what you want for Christmas," Don said as they dug. "I bet you a quarter I can guess."

Susan didn't even look up. She just kept digging around in the nest with her stick.

"A new doll."

"Nope."

"Lilly's getting kind of old. You want a new doll to play with."

"Nope."

Susan reached in and pulled something from the pile of twigs and nut shells. "Look—a penny."

Don inspected it. "That's not a penny. It's an old nickel—a buffalo nickel. See . . . there's the face of a president on one side, and there's a buffalo on the back."

Susan inspected the coin and then shoved it into Don's palm. "Put it in your pocket so I don't lose it."

When the pack-rat nest was totally demolished, they moved on to another pile of rocks farther up the hill.

"I got it!" Don said. "You want a new Sunday-go-to-meetin' dress. Yeah. A new dress and new shoes for church."

"Nope. I done got a pretty dress."

"I *have* a pretty dress," Don corrected.

"You got one, too?" Susan gasped.

Don felt the heat rush to his face. Then he noticed the mischievous twinkle in Susan's eyes. "I was correcting you, like Mom does," he said. "Don't get smart with me, or I'll swap ends with ya."

"Okay." Susan giggled. "I have a pretty dress."

"How about your shoes? They're a little tight, aren't they?"

"They're pretty, too. They're blue like my dress."

Don sighed.

A squirrel began scampering toward a tree. When I howled and took after it, they followed. Don saw it before Susan did and pointed it out to her. Then he told her to stay where she was, while he and I walked around the trunk. The squirrel tried to hide by circling to keep the tree between us.

That way Susan could get a good look when he crept around to her side.

"You probably don't want a toy," Don called from the other side of the tree. "Maybe you want a game, something you and I can play. Maybe something for the whole family. Parcheesi? Monopoly? Yeah. A game."

Susan's nose crinkled up.

"Then what do you want?" Don roared.

Susan's bottom lip started to quiver. Don rushed toward her.

I could smell and *feel* the mad on him. But it wasn't a mad like last night when Rex Covington said Dad was a coward. He wasn't mad at Susan. It was a different kind of mad.

Don was still mad but in control of it. Instead of stomping on something, he swooped Susan up in his arms and snuggled her against him. Then he spun her around and kissed her cheeks until she started giggling.

"I didn't mean to yell at you," he soothed. "You just don't get it. You *have* to tell somebody what you want. Even Santa can't hear, unless you say it out loud."

"I did said it out loud—"

"I did *say* it out loud," Don corrected.

"I say it out loud when I tell Santa. I say it every night, right after I say my prayers."

Don started to say something; but the sound of Mom's voice calling them to the house stopped him. Holding Susan's hand, he helped her down the hill as they walked back to the house.

"Tell you what," he said. "How about tonight we sit down and write Santa a letter? We'll tell him everything we want."

"But if we do that, I won't know for sure if the present came from Santa or from one of Santa's helpers."

That mad-at-Don feeling rippled through him again. He took a deep breath.

"There's even one thing I haven't told Mom and Dad that *I* want for Christmas. We'll both sit in your room, and I'll write my letter and help you write yours. Then tomorrow we'll take them to the post office. We won't let Mom or Dad or any of Santa's helpers see it. We'll just mail them to him. How does that sound?"

Susan smiled.

Don felt right proud of himself.

My tail wagged.

Chapter
11

When Don's dad had come back from the navy, he'd brought some things with him. His old uniform hung in the closet with his dress whites next to it, all pressed and neat. His shoes were there, too, all spit-polished and shiny as could be. He'd also brought two huge white cotton sea bags. Kyle tried to tell Don that they were called duffel bags, and they were supposed to be green instead of white. But Dad told him that Kyle's dad was in the army. *They* had green duffel bags. In the navy they were white, and they were sea bags.

Worn, tattered, and thin in a couple of spots, the sea bags *didn't* stay in the closet. Mom used them to haul clothes to the Laundromat on Main Street. Usually she had one sea bag stuffed clear to the brim and a small cloth sack for Susan to carry.

But Don saw both sea bags sitting by the front door.

On the walk back with Susan, he'd been thinking about how long it had been since he and Kyle had actually gone fishing, and had planned to ask Mom if he could go *for real* this time, while she and Susan were washing the clothes. But with two bags full of wash, he'd have to help carry.

When he first saw them, he thought about suggesting she take the pickup, but he already knew what her answer would be. She'd just say something like, "There's no sense wasting money on gasoline when the laundry in Devlin Hollow is just down the hill."

So he shook a dime out of his piggy bank and stuck it in his pocket. That way, after they were done with the wash, he could call Kyle from the pay phone in town. As long as Kyle wasn't grounded, they could meet at the lake and fish.

On the way down the trail, Mom let Susan get ahead of them. "You find out what she wants?" she whispered.

Don shook his head. "Not yet. But I think

we'll know tonight. Susan and me are going to write letters to Santa Claus."

"Susan and *I*," Mom corrected. Then she smiled. "Letter's a good idea. You're getting to be pretty sharp."

Don couldn't help but smile back.

Doing the laundry was boring! Especially when Don first got there. He helped Mom with the first load. When it was done, she and Susan loaded the washer again.

While they were waiting, he asked about going fishing. Just as he expected (and deserved), she asked if they were *really* going fishing this time. When he promised that the lake was the only place they would go, she agreed.

Don dug the dime out of his pocket. Head down, looking at the dime in his hand, he shoved on the laundry door.

The door shoved back.

He glanced up. Kyle stood on the opposite side of it with his nose and lips smushed against the glass, his eyes crossed. He was the goofiest-looking thing Don had ever seen. Don stepped aside. Still pressing his face against the glass, Kyle shoved the door open. Kyle's mom dragged two green duffel bags into the laundry.

"Quit it!" she scolded. "You're getting the glass all messy."

Tugging a third duffel bag, Kyle followed her.

"You get a bustin'?" Don whispered.

"Nope. You?"

"Nope."

"You grounded?" Kyle asked.

"Nope. You?"

"Nope."

And at almost the same exact instant, both boys looked at each other and asked. "Fishing?"

Like usual Susan wanted to go, too. *"No!"* Don snapped at her. The look on her face made him feel guilty, but having a little kid along was a pain. He always had to bait her hook and throw the line out for her, and the instant he turned his back, she'd start reeling it in. Then he'd have to cast it again and again. That left him hardly any time to fish.

Susan turned to Mom. "*Please*. Please make Don let me go with them."

Mom seemed to study the pleading look on Susan's face and the desperate look that Don gave. Finally she sighed and convinced Susan that she needed her help with the laundry.

It was four by the time Don, Kyle, and Frank got to the lake. Kyle set his tackle box and the jar of his dad's favorite stink-bait on the ground. "Think we're here too early?"

Don glanced at the sky. "Reckon we're okay. The fish ought to start hitting anytime now."

Kyle pulled out his pocketknife, cut the single hook off his line, and pulled a three-way from his tackle box. "You ask your dad about the weather? I bet the fish would really be biting if there was a cold front moving in."

"Forgot," Don answered, reaching out to borrow Kyle's knife so he could change hooks.

Kyle handed him the knife. "How does your dad do that, anyway?"

"Huh?"

"How does your dad do that?"

"Do what?"

"The weather. Most folks in Devlin Hollow are all the time asking him what the weather's gonna do. Lots of people don't have TV to get the weather report, but even the ones what do ask him. How does he know stuff like that?"

Don finished the knot, cut off the leftover line, then handed the pocketknife back to his friend. "I don't know. Funny thing about it, Dad don't know, either. I've asked him a couple of times. He says it's just a feeling—somethin' he can't explain. He just 'feels' when there's a change in the weather."

Don's first cast hit right about where he wanted it to. But when he threaded two worms on his old rod and reel, the line went sailing, and jerked to a sudden stop. It was so hard it almost yanked the rod out of his hand.

"Backlash," he muttered.

It took a good ten minutes of tugging and picking at the fishing line to get it untangled. He baited up again and used his thumb to adjust the pressure on this cast. The bait casting reel still spun a little fast, but this backlash only took him about three minutes to untangle. The third cast laid his line, in deep water, not far from his other one.

Frank sniffed both rods. Then he sniffed the tackle box, the can of worms, and Kyle's stink-bait. After that, he trotted back to start all over again.

"Sit down, Frank," Don scolded. "You keep trotting back and forth, you're gonna snag the lines. Get yourself all tangled up."

Frank looked at him and wagged his tail. Suddenly his ears perked, his nostrils flared, and his eyes seemed to focus on something behind them.

A brown Chevy station wagon was parked at the crest of the hill, with its tailgate down. A man was pulling something from inside the car. When he straightened to prop a couple of fishing rods against the car, Don could see him a little better. Tall and lean with dark hair, he looked about Dad's age or a little older. But Don couldn't really see him that well from here. When the man pulled a metal tackle box from the back and closed the rear of the station wagon, Don could finally see his face. Whoever he was, Don didn't recognize him.

Kyle propped his second rod against an old log and sat down.

Don motioned with a jerk of his head. "Who's that?"

"Who?" Kyle answered, looking all around.

"Up there." Don nodded again in the direction of the station wagon.

Kyle frowned. "Got no idea," he answered. "I've never saw him before."

Never seen him, Don corrected, just like his mother always did. Only he didn't say it out loud. Frank's hair was bristled to a ridge on his back. Stiff legs carried him as he trotted toward the man. Halfway down the hill, the man stopped. Frank sniffed from a distance. The ridge on his back smoothed down, and his tail began to wag.

"You boys doing any good?" the man called.

"Don't know yet." Kyle answered. "Just got our lines in the water."

"Looks like a good day for fishing."

"That's what we're hoping." Kyle didn't have to yell quite as loud, since the man was closer now. The man walked past them, put his things down, and then came back. Wagging his tail to beat the band, Frank bounced along beside him. When the man stopped in front of them and held out his hand, Kyle just sat there. Don hopped to his feet, like his dad had taught him, and looked the man square in the eye when he shook hands.

"I'm Samuel Devlin," he introduced himself.

"Don Franklin."

Don thought it was rude when Kyle just reached up from where he sat on the log. "I'm Kyle Benson."

"Devlin?" Don tilted his head to the side. "You any kin to Mrs. Devlin?"

"She's my mom." The man smiled; then *he* tilted *his* head to one side. "Don Franklin and Kyle Benson. Hmm . . . names are familiar. You two wouldn't happen to be the young gentlemen who mow Mom's lawn and help with the garden and flower beds during the summer?"

"Yes sir. That's us."

"Thought so," Mr. Devlin grinned. "She

thinks right highly of you. Says you're hard workers and mannerly. Tells me both of you see things that need doin' and do them without her having to tell you."

"She's a nice lady," Don said.

"You come for Christmas?" Kyle asked, not taking his eyes from his fishing line.

Mr. Devlin nodded. "Sort of. My brother is driving up from Houston and bringing his wife and daughter, and my wife and son. We're planning to spend Christmas, show the kids our old stomping grounds, then take Mom back home with us."

Don blinked. "Taking her back home . . . for a visit?"

Mr. Devlin pointed. "Better keep an eye on that rod. Think you got a little hit."

Don turned his attention to the rod tip. Mr. Devlin sat down beside him on the log. "Mom's getting up in years. We've been wanting her to come live with us for a while, but she doesn't want to leave her home. Tim and I call her at least once a week—usually more. She's still sharp as a tack—head works just fine. But her body's kind of giving out on her.

Fell last summer and messed up her knee. Didn't even tell us about it."

"I remember that," Kyle commented. "She usually comes outside to mess around in the garden and visit with us. Hardly came out at all during August."

Mr. Devlin nodded. "Then she got pneumonia in late October. We didn't even know she was in the hospital. When we called about four or five times and she didn't answer the phone . . . well . . . we got hold of Mrs. Taggert. Reckon Mom made her promise not to tell 'cause we practically had to pry it out of her to find out Mom was in the hospital over at McAlester." He snapped his fingers and pointed at the tip of Don's rod.

Don picked the rod up and yanked. Sure enough there was a fish. He could tell it was small because it didn't put up much fight when he reeled it in. The channel cat was only about eight inches long, so he pried the hook out of its mouth and gently pitched it back into the pond.

"Reckon it won't be easy to get your mom to leave her home."

"She's sure enough got a stubborn streak."

Mr. Devlin nodded. "But we promised her that we wouldn't sell the house. She's just coming for a long visit. Tim and I have a little spread outside Katy, Texas. Built her a house midway between each of ours. That way we can see to the place, drop by, and visit her every day, make sure she's all right."

"Hate to see her move away," Don admitted.

"Me too." Kyle agreed.

After a while Mr. Devlin made a grunting sound as he got up from the log. "Well, I'm getting a lot of visiting done but can't catch any fish if I got my mouth flapping. Looks like the cat fishing is a little slow. Think I'll see if I can catch me a bass or two. Nice to meet you boys. Like I said, Mom speaks highly of you both."

Don would miss Mrs. Devlin, but he could understand how her sons worried about her. Kyle caught a fish that was even smaller than the one Don caught. When Kyle pitched the fish back into the water, Don glanced to where Mr. Devlin was tying a plug onto his line. He also saw something else.

"You see what he's got?" Don whispered.

"What?"

"One of his reels. The bright silver one that's all closed up. That's a Zebco. One of those new spinning reels. Think I'll go ask him about it. See if he thinks it's as good as people say."

Chapter

People don't smell.

Well, that's not what I mean. People *do* smell. They just aren't *able* to smell. Yeah, that's it.

Sure they can pick up a few strong scents. They can tell when Mom's cooking fresh bread or something good for supper. Back when I was young and got sprayed by that skunk, they could smell that! Every time I so much as got close to them, they'd set up such a fuss, it made my head duck and my tail tuck. I didn't get to come inside for a month! They even fed me outside. Don would bring my food, set it down, then run for the door as if a whole pride of hungry mountain lions was chasing him.

But compared to us dogs, especially a bloodhound like me, they can't smell worth a flip. I can smell most everything.

On the way to the laundry with my family, I stopped by to say hello to some of my friends. Just from sniffing, I could tell old Slim, the pointer bird dog who lives with the Wilsons, wasn't feeling too well. His arthritis had been acting up, and he wasn't eating like he should. Benny, the Parsons' beagle, was happy as could be. Tina Parson had gotten over her measles and could come outside to play with him. Howler, who lived with the Yee family, got to go coon-hunting last night with his boy and the dad. They only treed one raccoon, but he felt like he'd done a good job and was right proud of himself.

I don't think people can smell feelings at all.

To me every feeling has a distinct odor. People try to hide the smells with their words or their faces, but the smells are still there.

There's the heavy smells. Those range from lies, mad, anger, clear up to rage. They're smells that make me feel like I'm being pushed down. Make it hard for me to breathe. Make me feel like running away.

Warm smells are on the other end. All sorts of things from carefree, relief, glad, excited, happy, affection, caring, clear up to love. I can smell them when I get a pat on the head or rubbed behind my ears. Those are the smells that make my tail thump the floor. Warm smells are soft and caring and gentle. But, thankfully, they're every bit as strong and powerful as the heavy smells. And with our family, there are a lot more of them.

Then there's about a million and one smells in between the heavy and the warm.

Worry hangs a little more on the heavy end. Want is more on the warm end. All those in-between smells can get pretty strong if people dwell on them too long.

The want on both Susan and Don kept getting stronger and stronger the closer we got to Christmas. I could smell *want*, but I didn't know what it was that either one of them wanted.

I smelled it when Don flipped through magazines with pictures of deer or fish on the front cover. There were a couple of times he even folded the edge of a page down and put the magazine back on the coffee table by Dad's end of the couch. It didn't take a genius to figure out his want had something to do with hunting or fishing. Susan was still a total mystery. But when that man showed up at the lake today, I *knew* what Don wanted. I knew it even before he started writing the list he was gonna make on the letters he and Susan would mail to Santa Claus.

Now this was fun!

Even though it was warm and pleasant outside, it was still good to get in the house. The first time Susan asked if I could sleep in her room, Mom and Dad said they'd think about it. We laid around in the living room while they watched their TV. Every once in a while, Mom or Dad would glance down at me, where I lay by the fireplace. When they figured I wasn't scratching at fleas, they finally told Susan okay.

A little after that, Don whispered something to Susan. She got up and went to her room. Susan bounced on her bed. I curled up next to her on the floor. Don brought pencil and paper from his room and knelt down by Susan's cedar chest.

"You want to go first?" he asked. "Or you want me to start?"

"You," Susan answered.

"Dear Santa," he wrote as he spoke. "Other than sneaking off to the miners' meeting the other night and fighting, I've been a pretty good boy this year. I know you can't get me everything I want, but here are some things I'd like to have. First off . . ."

Right from the get-go, I could tell that Don was saying a lot more words than he was writing. Since I couldn't read, I just had to guess at what words he was putting on his letter.

". . . I'd like a pair of high-top Converse All Stars. I think they'd keep me from twisting my ankles so much when I play basketball at school. That's what Jessie Cob wears. He's the best basketball player in high school. I really need a couple of new knit shirts for school, too. One or two of those pullover shirts. And I'd like a real tackle box for my fishing stuff. You know, one that has a lid and different compartments inside for hooks and weights and plugs. And I'd like a new pair of church shoes. The other ones don't hurt my feet, but they're sure lookin' shabby. And a Monopoly game. I played that a couple of times with Kyle and his family. It's fun. And a pair of wheat jeans—"

"What are those?" Susan interrupted.

Don shrugged. "Well, they're just like regular jeans, only sort of white or wheat-color. A lot of the guys at school are starting to wear them. They look pretty sharp."

Don checked his list and then made a big show

of looking around to make sure the door was shut. He motioned for Susan to come over and kneel beside him. I followed her.

"Okay," he whispered. "Now this is what I really, *really* want Santa to bring me. But you got to promise not to tell. Okay?"

"Okay," Susan whispered back.

He looked back at his list and smiled. "Please. Pretty please bring me one of those new Zebco spinning reels."

I knew that was all he wrote because he put his pencil down and kept talking. He told Susan that he and Kyle had met Samuel Devlin today when they were fishing. Then he told her all about the reel Mr. Devlin had. It didn't backlash. You could use bait, just like a regular reel, or plugs. Cast as many times as you wanted without worrying about getting tangled. According to Mr. Devlin, the new Zebco spinning reels were the most wonderful invention since toilet paper.

When Don was through talking, he folded his paper and put it inside another piece of paper. He licked that piece of paper and pressed it shut. Then on the front, he wrote something and stuck a tiny square piece of paper on the corner.

With a smile, he put a fresh sheet on the cedar chest, hugged Susan, and gave her a little kiss on the cheek.

"Okay. Your turn," he said

"Dear Santa"—Don wrote on the paper while she talked—"I have been pretty good this year. Sometimes I get mad at my friends at school, but I don't never be mean to them or try to beat them up like Don does. I want you—"

Don stopped writing. "Wait a second." He sighed and stared down at the paper for a moment. "How about we say, 'Sometimes I get mad at my friends at school, but I'm not mean to them'?"

"Okay."

"Okay." He finished writing. "Now go on from, 'I want you . . .'"

"I want you to bring me Raggedy Ann and a Raggedy Andy doll so Lilly and me—"

"And *I*," Don corrected.

". . . Lilly and *I* can have company when we have a tea party. And I want some paper dolls like I saw at the Ben Franklin store in McAlester, so I can dress them up and put lots of different clothes on them. And bring me a Far Cheesy game and—"

Don stopped writing again. He stared at his paper,

glanced over at Susan, then started at his paper again. Finally he smiled. Made a little snorting sound to keep from chuckling.

"*Parcheesi* game."

"I guess." Susan shrugged. "Is that the one with the dice and the little pieces you move around the board?"

Kind of clamping his lips together to keep from laughing, Don nodded. "That's *Parcheesi*. Not *Far Cheesy*. Okay?"

"Okay. Parcheesi game."

"And?" Don urged when Susan stopped. "And???"

Chapter
13

Don slammed the door so hard, he even scared himself. He didn't glance back to see if he'd broken something. He just stomped into the living room and threw himself onto the couch. The landing was so hard that Mom and Dad kind of bounced on either side of him.

"I'm gonna kill her. I don't care if she is my sister," he muttered. "I love her, but I'm gonna kill her anyway. I'm gonna beat her to a pulp. Dad can kill me right back. It don't matter. I don't care if the sheriff comes and takes me to jail. I'm gonna—"

Suddenly realizing how stupid and childish he sounded, Don took a deep breath. He sucked the air in until he couldn't hold any more, then let it out slowly, counting to ten inside his head like Mom had told him to do when he got mad.

He'd said stuff like that before. Things like he hated somebody, or he wanted to beat somebody to a pulp. Mom and Dad didn't like that kind of talk. He let his breath out slowly again and counted to ten a second time.

It was somewhat of a shock when Mom just glanced at him and very calmly said, "Don't kill your baby sister."

"Yeah," Dad added from the other side, without even looking away from the TV. "Something like that would really mess up our Christmas."

Don finally managed to close his mouth. He relaxed a little, too.

Mom leaned over and gently ruffled his hair.

"Wouldn't tell you?"

"No!" he snapped. Then with a sigh he added, "Got a whole list of stuff, Raggedy Ann and Raggedy Andy dolls, a Parcheesi game, paper dolls she can dress, new shoes that match her Sunday-go-to-meeting outfit. I really think she'd like a new dress, too. She mentioned it, only she didn't want me to write it down because she couldn't decide what color.

"But she wouldn't tell what she *really* wants Santa to bring her. She won't tell you! She won't tell Dad! She won't tell me! I told her that even Santa doesn't know unless she says it—*out loud!*"

A little jerk snapped Don's head up. He looked at Mom. "Wait. Wait." He tapped Dad's leg to make sure he was listening too. "This morning she *did* tell me that when she finishes her prayers, she *does* tell Santa out loud. I got it! I know what we could do. When she says her prayers, tonight, maybe I could—"

"Don." The tone of Mom's voice stopped him before he could get the rest of it out. "Eavesdropping on somebody's prayers isn't right."

With a sigh, he sank back into the couch. "I know. I know. I just can't figure out what else to do. Whatever it is she wants, it's really important to her. It's something she wants real bad. She's gonna be so disappointed if she don't get it."

"Doesn't."

"Huh?" Don frowned.

"*Doesn't* get it," Mom said.

Don just nodded. "I mean, it's gonna break her heart. She's gonna think Amy Covington was right all along. That'll make her feel downright rotten. Make it hard for her to believe in *anything*."

Dad leaned over and wrapped an arm around Don's shoulder.

"Disappointment is just part of life, son. Each and every one of us has to learn to handle it at some point."

"I know, Dad. But she's so young. Couldn't we just—"

"Some things we don't have any control over," Mom said. "We're going to McAlester tomorrow to finish our Christmas shopping. Keep an eye on her. Maybe we'll see a look in her eye when we're talking about presents and mention the right thing, but maybe we won't ever be able to figure it out. Either way it's not up to us. If it's time for Susan to face disappointment . . . then . . . well . . . it's time."

Don tossed and turned and fretted about his little sister instead of falling asleep. Behind the darkness of his closed eyes, he could see her sitting in front of the Christmas tree, all slumped over and trying to fight the tears back. She'd be heartbroken.

Then he remembered the BB gun he'd wanted so badly when he was eight. He didn't get that—yet he survived. Fact was, now that he thought back on it, all the thing would have ended up doing was getting him in trouble. If he'd gotten it, he'd probably have broken a window, or put somebody's eye out, or killed some poor bird and felt guilty about it for the rest of his life.

He rolled to his other side and thought of what his Dad had said about the Adamson Number One. He saw men working. The sound of timbers cracking. Men running, screaming, trying to get out. All those horrors inside his mind's eye made him sit up straight in bed. He wiped his forehead with the sleeve of his pajamas and tried to force the terrifying sights and sounds away from his mind.

He rolled onto his back and stared up at the ceiling for a moment before trying to force himself, once more, to get some sleep.

All Don could do was wish that tomorrow night would be better.

The way things started out, it didn't look like his wish would come true.

On the drive to McAlester, when they were in the stores, and on the drive back, they'd mentioned or pointed out almost everything under the sun that a six-year-old girl might want.

No smile. No bright eyes. No excitement. Nothing!

When they got home from shopping, and Dad turned the truck engine off, the phone was ringing. Mom hopped out to go answer it while the rest of the family started loading their arms with packages.

"It's for you, Delbert," she called. Once inside Dad dropped his load on the couch and picked up the phone. The serious look on his face froze them in their tracks.

"That was Keith Benson," he announced. "Two men from the Bureau of Mines came in today. Never dreamed they'd get here this quick. They started the inspection, so the mine will probably be closed until the day after Christmas."

The phone rang again. Mr. Leverett called with the same news. Then Kendall Washington.

Don and Mom finished unloading the truck.

Then Mark O'Ryan called. Then . . .

When Mrs. Taggert called, Dad asked that she let everyone else who called know that he already had the news.

Now that the phone had quit ringing, they sat down to put names on the different packages. Mom helped Susan with the gifts she was giving. And Don could swear that a couple of times he caught Mom and Dad both looking at her. It was the same look he gave Susan when she wouldn't tell what she really wanted for Christmas.

Tonight *had* to be better. The mine was always closed on Sundays and on Christmas. Tomorrow was Sunday. That's why they went shopping today. Monday, Dad would usually have to be back at the mine. None of the stores in McAlester were open on Sundays, so today was their last chance for Christmas shopping.

But for the first time he could ever remember, this year that stupid mine would be closed for three whole days. Tomorrow was Sunday, Christmas Eve was Monday, and Tuesday was . . . Don shook his head. No! Counting today, that was four days, not three. Dad didn't have to go in for the evening shift. For four whole days, Dad didn't have to go down in the earth. None of the miners did.

Don just knew he was gonna sleep like a baby tonight.

Don usually stayed up later than his little sister. But since he hadn't slept very well the night before, he went to bed just after she did. Frank curled up on the floor in Don's room. Don put on his pajamas and practically dove into bed. He closed his eyes and snuggled under the sheet.

Then . . .

Visions of Susan and Amy and Rex Covington hit him. He flopped to his side. He saw Susan sitting in the middle of all the wrapping paper, with tears dripping down her cheeks. He heard something. The sound came again. It was Frank. His rump sticking up in the air, Frank's front end was down so he could sniff under the crack at the bottom of the door.

Something was there.

On tiptoes Don crept across the room. He turned the doorknob, hoping it wouldn't creak when he opened it.

Mom stood there with her ear almost touching Susan's door. Don slipped back into bed.

Sleep came quick and easy that night. The only thought in Don's head was *not* to let Mom know that *he knew* how she found out what Susan wanted for Christmas.

Chapter

Something was going on. I just couldn't smell what.

It started last night. *That* I could smell.

Sneaky.

I smelled it on Don when he left Mom, Dad, and Susan watching *I Love Lucy*, and slipped into his room. He pulled a small box out of his pocket, opened it, smiled, then wrapped it in bright paper. From the other pocket, he pulled a bright, shiny new Barlow pocketknife, which he wrapped as well. Sneaky was heavy in our room. But when Don walked over and shook his piggy bank where he kept the money he'd been saving for a new lawnmower blade, he sighed. The sneaky faded away. Happy and right proud drifted to my nose.

Later that evening, I smelled sneaky again. And of all people . . . it was coming from Mom!

When I'd sniffed at Don's bedroom door, I first thought she was in the hall making sure Susan was tucked in and asleep. But the longer she stood there, the more sneaky I'd smelled. It wasn't a smell I was used to on her.

Don smelled it, too. Otherwise he wouldn't have been so quiet about tiptoeing across the room. He opened the door just a crack, then eased it shut. But when he crept back to his bed, all the worry and troubles seemed to slip away from him in an instant. He fell asleep so fast, I wasn't even curled beside the bed before I heard his breathing change to that soft, easy rhythm.

At breakfast all sorts of happy smells filled the kitchen. There was a lot of excited talking, too. Only it was soft, as if someone might hear. That kind of confused me because when they spoke, I thought *talk* was supposed to be heard. But through all the quiet talk, there was one word that came through as clear as a bell.

Kitten!

Just the word sent a chill up my back, clean from the tip of my tail to the tip of my nose. Maybe I hadn't heard it. Maybe it was another word. I lifted my ears. Listened. Hoped against hope that I hadn't heard . . .

The soft talk would rise, then lower to a nervous silence, only to get loud once more. Mostly their voices were hushed. Talk that was so soft even my big floppy ears could barely hear. And once more I heard that dreaded word . . .

Kitten!

When Susan's bare feet came padding down the hall, all the talk ended. She staggered in, and nothing but silence greeted her. She stopped and looked from one to the other. Instantly the talking started once more. Only this time, their chatter was about something completely different.

They talked about the weather. They talked about how warm it was; and although Dad said they were going to have a white Christmas, Don and Mom didn't believe him. They talked about how wonderful it was for Dad to have three more days off from the mine. Not the kind of talk that was anything like it had been before Susan came into the room.

Susan gave them a look. The way she frowned, and the way her mouth twisted up on one side, I could tell she was suspicious about the sudden silence. But when Mom put two whole-wheat pancakes on her plate, and Don scooted the pan of syrup in front of her, she wasn't suspicious anymore. She just grabbed her fork and dug in.

Once sure everyone was fed, Mom cut up the leftover pancakes for me. She even poured some of that delicious syrup over them. You talk about larrupin' good!!! When my people finished breakfast, Mom glanced up at the clock.

"Nine o'clock," she announced. "Let's get ready for church."

Everyone scurried off to their rooms. I followed Susan. When she started pulling her school clothes out, I figured they were getting ready to go off and leave me again. *Good time to go see Red,* I thought with a wag of my tail. Maybe spending some time with him would keep that horrid word—*kitten*—from echoing in my ears. Maybe he could help. I trotted to the back door and asked to be let outside.

I circled to the north and came in from the Watsons' yard. It was the only way the town dogs wouldn't spot me and start barking. Well, that and the fact that the wind was out of the south. Red's sense of smell wasn't as keen as mine—but almost. After all, he was a coonhound. Being downwind gave me an advantage. Pausing behind the lilac bush for a moment, I scanned the yard. Made sure he wasn't out and about, and finally spotted the bone.

Once sure it was all clear, I eased around the bush. Quieter than a cat sneaking up on a bird, one gentle step at a time, I crept across the yard. Keen eyes blinked and darted from side to side, watching for him to appear from some unseen hiding place. My ears perked up when I spotted his hind legs sticking out of his doghouse. He was lying flat on his back and sound asleep. Leaning forward I snatched the bone and curled my lip on one side.

"Mine!" I growled. Then I took off.

Red was awake and on his feet in an instant. He snarled, barked, and came charging through the doorway. I darted around the lilac bush. Red was hot on my heels. He kept up pretty well across the Watsons' yard, but halfway up the hill he started lagging behind. I stopped, laid the bone down, pinned it to the ground with both of my paws, and waited for him to catch up.

There had been times—back in Red's younger days—he would have chased me clear to the lake. But that's when his boy was still living at home, and he and his dad kept Red in good shape coon-hunting. Now that his boy had gone off to school, and the dad had spent so many years in the coal mine that the black dust made it hard for him to breathe, much less go hunting, Red didn't get to go coon-hunting, either. He was getting kind of out of shape. I was lucky. I still had kids to take care of.

Hair bristling from his ears to his tail, Red finally trotted up beside me.

"Mine," I growled, pinning the bone even tighter beneath my paws.

With that Red flopped down beside me. We visited awhile and basked in the warm winter sun. Part of the conversation was trying to recall which one of us had really found the bone first. Not that it mattered. To us whoever had it was who it belonged to. In a couple of days, or a week or so— about the time I forgot—Red would show up at my house and get it back.

When we parted company and I was carrying my trophy home, I couldn't keep from wondering where my family had gone. Yesterday they were gone. Today they were gone again. Only today was kind of different. The nice clothes they had on seemed familiar, the kind of clothes they wore one day almost every week.

I was about halfway up the hill when I suddenly remembered what I needed to tell Red. I dropped the bone and spun around. The old coonhound was about halfway down the hill. When I barked for him to stop, he turned toward me. I trotted to meet him so he wouldn't have to walk so far. Glancing back at the bone, I decided there was no need to worry. If he tried to make a run for it, there wasn't a doubt in my mind that I could beat him. Standing real still, I let Red circle and sniff.

Suddenly both his ears perked up. Both of his eyes popped as big around as Mom's pancakes.

"What did you say!?"

"A kitten," I repeated with my best scent.

Red's haunches seemed to fold in under him. He sank down on his rump and ended up sitting smack dab on his tail. He had to raise up a bit to get it uncrumpled.

"You're kidding. That's horrible!"

"I know." I shook my head until my ears flopped. "I just don't know what to do about it. I love my Susan but . . . but . . ."

He nodded.

Now *my* haunches folded. I managed *not* to sit on my tail, but I felt like my hind legs just gave way.

"That's bad, Frank. Real bad." Head lowered, Red's ears drooped so far forward that they almost covered his eyes. "I know you love your Susan. But kittens stink. They climb on you. They get into your food. They stick their claws into you when you're trying to sleep, and—"

"And?" I urged.

"And . . . worst of all . . . they grow up to be . . . to be . . ."

The word was almost too nasty for him to say.

"They grow up to be . . . *cats!!!*"

Chapter
15

On the way back from church, Don spotted Frank on the hill to the left of the dam. He and another dog were about thirty yards off the path. It struck him as a bit odd. With that bloodhound nose of his, Frank almost always knew he and Susan were around long before they so much as spotted him. But the old hound didn't seem to have the slightest idea they were there.

Frank was lying flat on his belly with both paws covering his ears and eyes. Another dog stood over him. It was a reddish-brown coonhound. Don thought it was the Goodmans' dog, only he wasn't sure. As still as Frank was, and with that other dog towering above him, Don thought for a second that there must have been a fight. Only the other dog didn't seem mad or mean or anything like that. He just stood there, looking down at Frank.

Dad paused a moment and motioned with a nod of his head. "Isn't that Frank?"

"Think so," Don answered. He felt his muscles tense. "Is he all right?"

Dad shrugged. "Can't tell. Doesn't seem like a fight. Maybe he's sick or something."

Right about then the coonhound spotted them walking up the path toward the dam. He leaned over and nudged Frank with his nose. Instantly Frank's head sprang up. He hopped to his feet and trotted toward them.

As far as Don could tell, Frank looked fine. There was still something strange going on. It took him a second or two to figure it out. Usually Frank's tail swayed back and forth when he trotted to greet them. As Frank came down the hill, his tail was tucked tight against his rump. Weird. His tail wagged when he reached them. Then it tucked again, when he stretched up to smell each one. He even sniffed at the old Bible that Mom's grandmother had given her. It was the one she always carried to church. He circled to sniff Susan, then came back for one more snort at Mom's Bible. In the blink of an eye, Frank was back to his usual self, tail up and swaying in the breeze as he led the way home.

They were almost to the place where the path split, where the left fork went over the dam and up the hill to the mine, and where the right fork went to their house, when Don heard the sound. Everyone stopped.

It was a dog barking. He finally spotted the coonhound. It barked a second time, then leaned over and picked something up. Don couldn't tell for sure what it was. Looked like a bone or something. Head high as a coyote baying at the moon, the coonhound lifted the bone in the air. Then he pranced off down the hill. Don had never seen a dog "prance" before. But he couldn't think of any other way to describe it.

When he glanced down, he saw a ridge of bristled hair that went from Frank's ears clean to the tip of his tail. Don watched him a second. The ridge flattened. His tail started to wag. And for just an instant, Don could swear he saw his bloodhound smile.

He couldn't keep a little chuckle from slipping out at the silly thought. *Dogs can't smile*, Don told himself. *They can't frown, either. They're just dogs. Still* . . . He shook his head and laughed again. *You sure come up with some dumb thoughts, sometimes. Thinking a dog can smile is just about as stupid as thinking dogs can talk. You're letting your imagination get away from you.*

Mom had started the Sunday roast before they left. She handed her Bible to Susan while she turned the roast with her long fork and added a bit more water. Then everyone headed to their rooms to change out of their Sunday clothes. Don had only taken a couple of steps when he felt a tug on his shirttail. Mom put a finger to her lips, shushing him until Susan disappeared into her room.

"After dinner I need you to take Susan someplace for a few minutes," she whispered. "Maybe half an hour or so. I've got some people to call, and your dad's gonna make an excuse to get out of the house. McAlester has a Sunday paper, but we don't get it here in Devlin Hollow until Monday. He's gonna drive over and pick one up. See if he can find an advertisement for anyone who has kittens for sale."

Smiling, Don nodded and scurried off to change.

Don felt downright miserable after dinner. He guessed that Dad had eaten too much, too, because he'd planned to leave for McAlester right after lunch but was still sitting on the couch, snoozing off and on, and watching the TV. Don was on the floor, but he couldn't nap like Dad had been doing. When he tried lying on his back, he felt like he could hardly breathe. When he rolled on his stomach, he couldn't get comfortable either.

Lying there he saw Mom nudge Dad's foot with hers. When he didn't stir, she kicked him. Dad's eyes flashed wide. He sat up straight on the couch and cleared his throat.

"Didn't you have to go pick up something for the machine shop at the mine?"

Dad closed his eyes, then they flashed open again. "Almost forgot." He yawned. Then struggling to his feet, he added, "Guess I better drive over there."

Don could see Frank curled up on the floor between Mom and Dad. When Mom asked Dad if he was supposed to pick up something, Frank sniffed her leg and gave her a funny look. When Dad answered, Frank sniffed his leg and gave *him* a funny look. It was almost like he could tell they were lying.

Don rolled his eyes. *There you go again,* he thought. *Thinking that dumb old dog can actually tell they're making up stuff. How in the world do you get such crazy ideas stuck in your head?*

With a moan, Don struggled to his feet. "I feel like I'm about to blow up," he admitted. "Think I'll go for a walk. See if there are any deer tracks around."

Frank stood up, sniffed, and looked over the coffee table at Don with that same funny look he'd given Mom and Dad, but he ignored it. When Susan didn't respond, he nudged her with his foot.

"You wanna go with me, squirt?"

Susan just lay on the rug in front of the fireplace. "I'm sleepy."

"Better go with him," Dad said. "It's fixin'

to turn cold. Might as well enjoy this nice weather while it lasts."

The whole family looked at him.

With a smile and a shrug, Dad added, "Tomorrow or Christmas Day." That's all he said. It was all he needed to say.

With Frank leading the way, Don and Susan headed toward the creek that flowed into the lake. Don kept looking at the sky, thinking about what Dad had said about the weather and how nobody so much as questioned him.

Don had been six when they'd moved to Oklahoma from Pennsylvania. He didn't remember all that much about Pennsylvania. He did remember the snow. There was a lot more of it, it was deeper, and it stayed longer than when it snowed here in Oklahoma. But that's about all he remembered.

What he *did* remember was the first year they had moved here.

Dad had come home from the mine one day and told them that there was a storm coming. But the weather was clear as glass, and there was no wind. Nothing happened that night or the next day. But when Dad came home the following afternoon, he made them fix bed-rolls, had Mom pack a sack lunch, and they spent the night in the mine.

It was the first time Don had ever gotten to go down in a mine. He couldn't remember much of it—there was a hole, then a tunnel and a funny smell. When they came out of the mine the next morning, folks were talking about a twister.

Homes in McAlester and Krebs had been damaged. People had been hurt, but there were no deaths. When they got home, Mom and Dad had to replace boards on the southwest corner of the house and put new shingles on the roof. A willow tree that stood at the corner of the house was bent and twisted so much it almost seemed to lie down.

Dad never could explain how he knew there was a storm coming. But after that, Don and Mom never questioned him. They just accepted that Dad knew when something with the weather was going to change.

Don and Susan were coming back from hunting for tracks along the creek when Dad's truck pulled up. While they'd seen lots of coon and skunk tracks, they'd only seen a few deer tracks. It didn't matter. Getting Susan out of the house so Mom could talk on the phone was what was important.

Mom was in the kitchen. Making sure he was between Susan and her, Don smiled and wiggled his eyebrows.

"Dad find what he was looking for?"

Mom didn't smile back. "Nope. Probably have to go back tomorrow."

"Is it a Christmas present?" Susan asked.

Mom forced a smile, then leaned around Don so she could see her. "No, dear. Just something for the mine. Oh, by the way, I need you to help me with the cake and corn-bread dressing tomorrow. Okay?"

Susan's smile almost lit up the whole room. "Can we make cookies, too?"

"Maybe." Mom smiled back at her. "Don, I'm going to need you to do a couple of errands for me tomorrow. Okay?"

"Yes, ma'am."

Don waited patiently until Susan scurried off to her room. When he heard the door close, he leaned toward Mom.

"Dad didn't have any luck?"

Mom shook her head. "No. Molly Taggert's helping. Guess she's been asking everybody who rings in because she's called me back five times."

"And?" Don urged.

"And . . ." Mom shrugged. "Nothing. The Blevins' cat had a litter, but they've already given them away. Beth Salyer's cat had a litter two days ago, but they're way too young to be weaned. She also called a couple of dairy farmers on the far side of the mine, but neither of them answered the phone when she called. They've either gone someplace or out milking the cows.

"That's where you come in. Tomorrow morning . . ."

Chapter

here in the world have you two been?" Mom asked the next day.

Mom's frown almost made my tail tuck under, but the anticipation in her voice kept it wagging. Then— when Don said, "There's not a kitten in the whole country"—well . . . my tail didn't know what to do.

Part of me was happy that we hadn't found a kitten. After all a kitten was just a baby cat. From my dealings with cats, I'd learned a long time ago that they were best left alone. Even if you're just trying to say howdy or make friends with them, they either spit in your eye, scratch your nose and ears—or both!

On the other hand, Susan wanted a kitten something fierce. Mom, Dad, and Don wanted one for her. They didn't want her to be sad on Christmas. *I* didn't want her to be sad, either.

So my tail just hung there, halfway between tucked and wagging, like it was frozen in midswing.

"We stopped at the Vaughn place first," Don explained. "Mr. Vaughn wasn't home. Went to pick up his kids and their family from the bus station in Oklahoma City. But Mrs. Vaughn told me they didn't have any kittens. We went to the Nelson farm next. Before we left, you told me he might be a little . . . a little . . ."

"Cantankerous?" Mom helped out.

"Not cantankerous. He was downright crotchety." Then with a smile, Don added, "At first."

Mom smiled back. "So what happened?"

"Mrs. Nelson sent me to the barn where her husband was working. When I found him, he was pounding on his tractor. I said, 'howdy,' and he just looked up and asked, 'What do you want?' It was more like a snarl. Kinda scared me. Frank and I were both ready to take off running. I finally managed to get out that we were looking for a kitten. Then he up and asks, 'Why in the world would you want a stinkin' cat?'

"When he found out that it was a Christmas present for my little sister, and she was only six years old . . . well, he was a completely different person."

"The Nelsons are good people." Mom nodded. "But they come off as cranky or cantankerous or downright mean at first—you know, till they get to know you. If they find out people are in need, they'll give you the shirts off their backs. Do anything and everything under the sun to help you out."

"That was Mr. Nelson, all right." Don almost laughed out loud. "When he found out that the kitten was a Christmas present for a little girl, he helped me search every inch of the hay barn, the sheds, even their storm cellar. When we didn't find any kittens, he loaded me and Frank in his pickup, and we started driving. I bet we stopped at every farm from here to . . ."

I didn't hear the rest of his story 'cause right about then I started sneezing. Four or five popped out in a row. I shook my head until my ears flopped, but just when I thought I was done, it started in again.

They let me outside. I was glad about that. There wasn't any need to hear Don's story. After all I was with him the whole time.

Riding in the back of that pickup truck had been fun. Feeling the air rush past was something I've always loved. But every time we stopped at a farm, Don and the farmer and I hunted for a kitten. All that sniffing around in the barns got my nose clogged up with dust and alfalfa leaves. Although there were no kittens to be found, there *were* lots of cats! The smell of them seemed to cling to the inside of my nose.

A breath of fresh air was just what I needed. Finally my nose started to clear.

First thing I noticed were the raccoons. Though I loved sleeping inside, that meant there was no one left outside to protect the place. I could tell that two raccoons had come the first night, then three the second. They crawled into the trash can and even the burning barrel. They were sure to be back tonight. I'd stay outside to run them off. Otherwise, they'd get so brazen, they'd start tearing something apart or messing up the place.

I sniffed around a bit more. My nose was almost back to normal. That's when I smelled it. The scent was faint on the soft south breeze. A man. Stink-bait. I shook my head. No. It wasn't stink-bait. It didn't smell strong enough. Maybe it was dough-bait. I raised my head and sniffed again.

Somebody was at the lake. From this far away,

and with the scent of cat still lingering in my nose, I couldn't tell who. But it just might be . . .

The corners of my mouth tugged until my face was probably as tight as a young pup's. Maybe it was that Devlin guy. And if it was . . .

Maybe—just maybe—it was worth a try.

Chapter
17

Dad was usually tired when he came home
from digging coal all day. But when he drove in
a little after sundown . . . well . . . Don didn't
think he'd ever seen him look so worn out. The
corners of his mouth drooped so much, it
reminded Don of Frank's jowls. Dad's brow
was wrinkled and even the lines at the sides of
his eyes (Mom called them his laugh lines)
seemed to slope down instead of up. Along
with all that, his feet seemed heavy as he lum-
bered up onto the porch, taking the steps one
at a time.

Mom met him at the door. She put a finger
to her lips to let him know Susan was taking
a nap. Then she gave him a big hug and kissed
him on the cheek. Both glanced around and
motioned Don to follow them outside.

"No luck with the newspaper?" she asked.

Dad just stared at the ground and shook his head. "Didn't find a 'for sale' ad in the newspaper for kittens. Didn't find a 'free kittens to a good home' ad. Absolutely nothing."

Mom frowned. "Then where have you been all this time?"

Dad sighed and sat down on the step. "Been going door to door. Started out at the feed store. Figured they always have a few cats around to keep the mice out of the grain. Had cats but no kittens. Then I just started driving up and down the streets. Knocked on people's doors, asked if they had any kittens or knew any one of their neighbors who might. On the way home, I stopped by farms." He glanced up at Don. "Last few places I stopped, they told me Farmer Nelson, along with a boy and a bloodhound, had already been asking about kittens. That's when I finally gave it up and came on home."

Don sat on the step beside him. Mom was on the other side. Dad patted her knee.

"You do any good here?" he asked.

Mom shook her head. "No kitten. But I tell you what—that Molly Taggert has tried her best. What did you call it in the navy—going above and beyond the call of duty?"

Dad nodded.

"You know how she has to keep a log of long-distance calls and pay-phone calls?"

Dad nodded again.

"Well she made up a separate logbook. She wrote down everyone who called through her switchboard and asked them if they had a kitten or knew anyone who did. She kept me posted. Then about thirty minutes ago, she called and said she had spoken to everyone in town except for five people. She just got through calling them. The Bensons were out of town, visiting relatives. So were the Grandons. Molly called their neighbors and had them see if they could find any cats at their places. Then she called the Lewises, the Koches, and the Bixlers."

Mom glanced up at the sky and shook her head. "I used to get irritated with that woman for listening in on conversations. Right now I feel ashamed of myself. She tried everything in the world to help us find a kitten for Susan. Talked to every single person in the whole valley. I promise—I'll never think bad thoughts about her again. She's a regular saint."

"What y'all talking about? Who's a saint?"

The screen door bounced shut, and all three of them jumped, their heads jerking around so hard it's a wonder they didn't get whiplash. Yawning and rubbing the sleep from her eyes, Susan waddled out to sit with them on the steps.

"We were . . . uh . . . we were just talking about Saint Nicholas," Mom lied. "You know the book I read every Christmas Eve? Its original title—you know when people first started reading it in newspapers and stuff—it used to be called *A Visit from Saint Nicholas.*"

"Yeah," Dad agreed. "Saint Nicholas is another name for Santa Claus. That's what they called him back when we were your age. Reckon it's been a hard year for old Saint Nick. Warm as it's been, his sled probably can't go as fast as usual without the snow to slide on. Then there's all the people. There's a whole lot more folks living in this old world than when I was a kid. It's a downright miracle that he can get to as many of them as he does."

Susan's bottom lip stuck out. "You mean Santa might not come this year?"

"Santa will come," Mom assured Susan, reaching out to hug her close. "It's just . . . well, we might not get every single present that we want."

"That's okay," Don added quickly. "Susan and I understand. We're old enough to know that Santa can't always get us everything. But I bet what he can't get this year, he'll be sure to bring next Christmas. All we have to do is just keep believing in him."

Dad made a grunting sound when he got up from the step. "I'm starving. Let's go eat supper."

Supper was pretty light on Christmas Eve. Mom had saved some of the roast. She cut it up and mixed it with carrots, potatoes, and onions to make stew. It was good. But even hungry as he was, Don tried not to eat too much. He had to save room for Christmas dinner.

There were four pans of corn bread baking in the oven; and as soon as supper was finished, Mom took the pans out of the oven to cool. When they were done with the dishes, Don helped break the corn bread into little pieces for the dressing.

After a bit, Don went to the living room. It was his last chance. Though it seemed useless, he just had to try one more time to make sure they knew what he wanted for Christmas. He got *Field and Stream* from the end table beside the couch. For three weeks, he had kept moving it so it was always on top of the magazine pile, open to the page with the advertisement for the Zebco spinning reel. That way Mom and Dad couldn't help but notice it. At least that's what he hoped.

But this time—just like every time he went to check—it seemed to be buried deeper and deeper in the stack.

It was close to bedtime when Mom and Susan finished with the sweet rolls and took their baths. When they came back to the living room, Mom brought an old copy of *The Night Before Christmas*. The pictures inside were kind of funny-looking—not like newer books. Don couldn't even think of a word to describe why they looked different. They just did. The cover was old and tattered, too. But the book was still extra-special to Mom because her grandmother got it when she was a little girl—about Susan's age. She had passed it on to Mom, who in turn would pass it on to Susan.

Mom and Dad sat on the couch. Dad pushed the coffee table back with his feet, so there was enough room near them for Susan and Don. After Don plugged in the lights on the Christmas tree, he nestled on the floor, resting his arm and head against Dad's leg. Once everyone was settled and the star shone bright at the top of the tree, Mom opened her book and began:

Twas the night before Christmas, when
    all through the house
Not a creature was stirring, not even a
    mouse.
The stockings were hung by the mantel
    with care,
In hopes that Saint Nicholas soon
    would be there.

*The children were nestled all snug in
      their beds,
While visions of sugarplums danced in
      their heads.
And mamma in her 'kerchief, and I in
      my cap,
Had just settled our brains for a long
      winter's nap.*

*When out on the lawn there arose such
      a clatter,
I sprang from the bed—*

That's as far as Mom got on account of the clatter on their *own* lawn.

They didn't spring from the couch to see what was the matter, they ran over one another to see what was going on. There was a bang or crash against the front door. Growling. A man yelling. A dog snarling. More yelling.

Then the distinct sound of Frank's bark. Then his growl. It wasn't one of his gentle growls, either. It was mean and threatening.

Mom and Susan rushed to the front windows to peek through the shades. Dad and

Don sprinted to the front door. Dad got there first and yanked it open.

"What's going on out here?" he demanded. "Who's there?"

A man stood about fifteen feet from the house, just barely in the porch's light. He held up his hands, showing that he meant no harm.

"Sorry," he called. "Didn't mean to startle you folks. Is that your dog?"

Dad glanced down at Frank.

"He's our dog. Why?"

Don looked down. Frank had something pinned beneath his paws. Teeth bared, he snarled as if guarding the thing with his life. Don blinked. Then he blinked again, not quite able to believe what it was that Frank was protecting.

Chapter

 or the life of me, I couldn't understand the fuss.

First off the guy followed me all the way home. I expected him to bark (I mean yell) and chase me for a little ways. That's how Red and I always played. It was part of the game—pretend to trail for a while, then go back home.

But all the way???

He would have never found me if the fishing line hadn't snagged on that tree. The string led him right to our front door.

And where did he get off telling my family I *stole* his Zebco rod and reel?

He wasn't using it. He'd left it leaning against the back of his station wagon while he fished with his other rod. That meant it was up for grabs. Why not let Don play with it for a while? Then when he wasn't using it, the guy was welcome to come and take it back.

People just don't know how to share.

He even called me names. I was *not* a thief!

My family got onto me. Dad scolded me. Don practically dragged me inside. Even Mom yelled at me. I guess she didn't like me climbing on the couch so I could bark out the front window and tell the man it was not his turn to use the rod and reel.

It just wasn't fair.

After things settled down a bit, Don stood by the front door, and I quit barking so we could listen. The man apologized to Dad for not introducing himself. He said his name was Samuel Devlin. Dad said that he figured as much because Don had mentioned meeting him the other night at the lake. Then the man said how much his mom liked Don and Kyle, and how she'd really miss them when she went to Texas. Mr. Devlin told Dad how she was always saying what nice boys they were, how well they did her lawn, and how neat and pretty it looked when they were finished.

Then Dad introduced himself, and he and the

man sat on the front step to talk, while the man started winding all the fishing line back onto the shiny silver reel. Their tone was light and cordial. Even the smells that drifted through the front screen were friendly instead of mad.

"Mr. Franklin," he said, turning to shake Dad's hand, "I really am sorry for startling you and your family. I saw a dog run off with my rod and reel. I guess I was just so intent on chasing him down, I didn't even think."

"No problem," Dad laughed. "I don't have any idea what got into old Frank. He's a good dog. Never done *anything* like this before. I'm just glad you got your rod and reel back. Oh, and by the way . . . it's Delbert . . . not Mr. Franklin."

They shook hands again, and Mr. Devlin smiled. "My friends call me Sam. Good to meet you, Delbert." He turned and started back toward the lake.

Then . . . suddenly . . . he stopped, almost frozen, as if he was about to step on a snake or something. Ever so slowly, he turned. The smile was gone. The smell that came from him was more excited than angry.

"Did you say *Delbert*? Delbert Franklin?"

"Yes," Dad answered.

The man stared at Dad for a long time. I could tell by the way Dad shifted his weight from one paw—I mean foot—to the other, that the look made him a little nervous. It didn't bother me, though. The smell that came from Mr. Devlin was excited. Happy. "Delbert Franklin?" he repeated one last time. "Catfish were biting real good tonight," he said. "Reckon it's the full moon, or you think there might be some other reason?"

Dad folded his arms. "Doubt it. New moon's better for fishing than a full moon. It's probably the cold front that's coming in. Fish bite better right before a front."

"Snow?"

Dad glanced at the moon. "Probably. No blizzard or anything like that. Maybe an inch or two. Why? What are you driving at, Sam?"

"You're from Pennsylvania. A little town called Paxton, up north of Harrisonville."

Frowning, Dad nodded. "Born there. Grew up in Powells Valley."

"You and your dad were coal miners, but your mom and dad both passed away while you were in the navy. You *were* in the navy, weren't you?"

Dad's mouth was open now. Only he wasn't saying anything. He just nodded.

"Served on a light cruiser called the *U.S.S. St. Louis*, right?"

Dad nodded again.

"No matter what they threw at her, they never could sink the Lucky Lou."

Dad's eyes flashed. When he repeated the name, "Lucky Lou," the tone of pride in his voice made my tail thump the couch. "You on the Lucky Lou?" Dad asked. "Were you navy?"

Mr. Devlin shook his head. "Army. But I have a man who works with us at our oil company who served on her. You don't happen to recall a fella by the name of James Wallace?"

Dad stared at him.

"Think he was a chief," Mr. Devlin added.

"His first name was James, but there were two James Wallaces on the Lucky Lou." Dad smiled. "So he went by his middle name, which was—"

"Lewis," Mr. Devlin interrupted. "That's because he said Lewis was his good-luck charm. Lewis on the *St. Louis* made both of them Lucky Lou's. And he was a master chief—"

"When we started out," Dad agreed. Now it was he who interrupted Mr. Devlin. "By the end of the war, he was a lieutenant commander." Dad stopped talking and frowned at Mr. Devlin for a moment. "What's all this about? How come you know so much about me, and why—"

"My brother, Tim, and I own an oil company in Houston," he began. "Lewis has been with us almost from the beginning. The three of us have hunted all over Pennsylvania and West Virginia, checked with every coal-mining operation we could, trying to find the Delbert Franklin who'd been a coal miner in Pennsylvania. Never dreamed you moved to Oklahoma. Can't believe it. Right here in Devlin Hollow. Not more than two miles from Mom's house. Spent years trying to find you, and you were right under our noses, all the time."

"Why were you trying to find me?"

I'd never smelled Dad so confused.

"Lewis heads up our offshore drilling operations. He told us the one person in the whole world who he needed, was a man by the name of Delbert Franklin." He glanced at his watch. "You mind walking with me back to the lake? I'll tell you all about it."

I really wanted to know what was going on. Leaping from the couch, I rushed to the door and whined. But Mom wouldn't let me go.

Chapter

19

Don couldn't believe Dad wouldn't let him go.

He closed the front door and stomped back to the couch. Wagging his tail, Frank trotted over and put a paw on his knee. Don glared down at him.

"What in the world's gotten into you, dog? Stealing a man's fishing rod, growling, and barking. Get over there! Go lay down!"

Frank tucked his tail and curled up in front of the fireplace. Don folded his arms and pouted.

He didn't pout for very long.

When he glanced over at Frank, it looked like the old bloodhound was pouting, too. Then he remembered seeing him yesterday. How he was all fuzzed-up at the coonhound. He recalled that when the dog trotted off with that bone, he almost thought Frank was smiling.

Dogs can't smile, he told himself. *Dogs*

can't pout, either. Just the thought chased the scowl from his face. It almost made him laugh. Then he got to thinking about the Zebco reel. The thing was so close, he could almost touch it. Frank must have . . .

Don shook his head. *No! It couldn't be. How would that dumb dog know how bad I want a Zebco reel for Christmas? He's just a dog. He couldn't—*

"Guess you two best be off to bed," Mom said. "Ten-fifteen. Way past your bedtime."

"No!" Susan snapped.

Mom's eyebrows arched. "What did you say, young lady?"

Don cringed. *You didn't say no to Mom or Dad. Leastwise not in that tone of voice.*

Susan must have remembered, too. She kind of ducked her head. "We haven't heard the book," she said softly, almost whispering. "We *always* listen to the story on Christmas Eve."

Mom sighed. "Okay. I'll finish it, then—"

"*No!*" Susan snapped again.

Mom's eyes flashed. Frank tucked his tail.

"Young lady! If you ever use that tone with me, again, I'll—"

"But Mom. You don't understand. Dad's not here." Tears began to gather at the bottom of her eyes. "We always read the book *together*. Our whole family. It's not Christmas without everybody, and"—more tears—"and Santa won't come"—the tears spilled over and raced down her cheeks—"and only Santa knows what I really want." Sobbing she buried her head in Mom's lap.

"Tell you what." Mom sniffed. "It's ten-fifteen. If your father's not back by eleven, both of you are going to bed, with or without the story. There will be no argument. Understand?"

Don could see the slight movement when Susan nodded her head. As Mom caressed Susan's hair, Don noticed that she kept looking at the clock almost as often as he did.

The whole family listened to *The Night Before Christmas*.

Of course, it was way past eleven before they got to bed. Dad came back from the lake about ten-forty. But everyone—even Mom— simply *had to know* what Mr. Devlin wanted.

"Sam and his brother want me to come to work for their oil company."

Mom's mouth fell open. "You don't know the first thing about oil wells."

Dad laughed. "That's exactly what I told him! But he said it didn't matter. He wants me to work with Lewis on the offshore rigs."

Mom looked worried. "So what are you supposed to do?"

"They want me to be their weatherman."

"That's all?"

Dad shrugged. "That's it. They need to know if there's a storm coming and how bad it's liable to be."

"And this is all from what Lewis told them? From back in the war?"

"Lewis remembers when I talked Captain Campbell into taking the ship through a typhoon after a battle. There were Japanese subs all around, and he figures I saved the ship when I told the captain the storm wouldn't be that strong.

"I was a gunnery mate, but I spent more time on the bridge than I did behind my gun. Found lots of storms for us to hide under."

"And you'll be working outside?" Mom broke in. "You don't have to go under the water, like those guys you told us about in the navy, the ones who had to wear the big bubble-like helmets and the lead boots? It's not dangerous or anything, right?"

"I won't be underwater. Mostly I'll be with Lewis, going from one rig to another, to see if everything's working okay.

"When they're getting a new rig and platform started, we might have to stay out a week or two. And during hurricane season, I probably wouldn't be home every night, either. So . . . to answer your question . . . it's not dangerous."

Mom straightened and kind of pushed her shoulders back. "I think we should do it!"

"Don't you want to know how much the job pays?"

Mom shook her head. "Not really. I think we should at least try it. You'll be working out in the fresh air. On the ocean. You won't have to go underneath the ground or under the water. Whatever he offers, I think you should take him up on it."

"He's already offered."

"Did you say yes?"

Dad shook his head. "Not without checking with you and the kids first."

"Far as I'm concerned, you need to march over to the Devlin place tomorrow, soon as we finish opening Christmas presents, and tell him you'll take the job."

"Me too." Susan added.

Don nodded. "Yeah. You don't know how much Mom and me worry—"

"Mom and *I*." She corrected.

". . . how much Mom and *I* worry about you when you're down in that mine."

Dad sighed and nestled back into the couch.

"He offered me fifteen hundred dollars starting salary." Mom's shoulders slumped. Then almost instantly she forced them back and sat up straighter than before.

"That's fine. That's uh . . . uh . . . it's a good offer."

Dad stared at her. She smiled.

"Really. Susan and Don are both in school. I've been needing something to do. I could get a job—you know, maybe a waitress job or something in a factory—like I did at the air-plane plant while you were in the war."

"I can mow lawns," Don said, trying to help Mom out. "I'm good at it. And I can do other things, too. Mom's right. You should take the job."

Dad shrugged. "Okay."

But he had a weird look and turned his face away.

That's when Mom read *The Night Before Christmas*.

When she was done, Dad patted Don on the knee. "Let's stack a few logs on the porch so we'll have dry wood for a fire tomorrow. Come with me and get an armload of kindling."

When they got to the door, they stopped. Dad nudged Don with an elbow. "Watch your mom," he whispered. Then louder he added, "Oh by the way, Alice, I almost forgot. Sam said they'd add another five hundred to the offer—if it really snows tonight. That will make it two thousand."

Mom smiled and nodded.

"And . . . another thing I forgot to men-tion." Dad turned his face away so she couldn't see. "That's two thousand . . . a month!"

Chapter

It startled me when Mom fell backward onto the couch.

I'd seen my family *sit* on the couch, *plop* on the couch. Don *bounced* on the couch when he was little, and Susan *hopped up and down* on the couch when no one was watching.

This was the first time I ever saw one of them *fall* on the couch. Mom landed so hard, it's a wonder she didn't bump her head.

I trotted over to sniff.

Her eyes were almost as big around as the pancakes she makes. They were glazed, too—almost glassy-looking. Her heart was going ninety-to-nothing, but her face was pale. And when I sniffed . . . well . . . there were so many smells, I couldn't sort them out. Excitement, disbelief, confusion, happiness, amazement. She was downright bewildered.

I sniffed again. Other than acting weird, falling on the couch, and looking funny, she was okay. Besides, there was work that needed to be done outside. I darted to the door so I could go with Dad and Don. The raccoons would be back tonight, and I had to keep them from spreading junk all over.

"Is two thousand a lot of money, Dad?" Don asked.

"Yes, Don. In my whole life, I never figured I'd ever have a job earning that much money."

"Is it more than you make at the mine?"

"We earn a little under seven thousand two hundred a year, digging coal. Foreman gets more than that, but not much."

"Then it's more. Right?"

Dad frowned at him. He laid his logs against the house beside the front door. Don piled his wood on top of them. "You do math in school. Two thousand a month. How many months in a year? You figure it out."

I followed them back for another load of firewood.

"That's more than twice as much, Dad," Don yelped.

"Way more. Now grab a load of kindling."

Don scraped a whole armload of small sticks

from what they called "the kindling pile." About halfway to the house, he stopped. "Is it really safe, or were you just telling Mom that so she wouldn't worry?"

"It's safe." Then Dad stopped to look back at his son. "Well, it's about as safe as anything else. When you get right down to it, just being alive isn't safe."

"Huh?" Don frowned. "What do you mean?"

They put their wood against the house. Then Dad sat and patted the porch step next to him. Don sat down. I lay at their feet.

"When I started coal mining with *my* dad, I was a lot like you and your mom. Every time I went down in the earth, it scared me. Always worrying about a cave-in or an explosion. Being trapped in the dark with no air. Guess that's why I signed up for the navy when the war started. The army boys were taught how to dig foxholes, but I didn't like the thought of digging myself down in the ground. I wanted to be out in the open, out on a ship in the middle of the sea, with the fresh breeze and salt-spray blowing in my face. That sounded like paradise to me. Trouble was, on a ship there's no place to hide.

"So I figured maybe I wouldn't be so scared all

the time, if I had a place down under the deck where I could hide.

"I never thought much about the enemy ships or subs—not until July six. The Lucky Lou took a torpedo aft but it didn't explode. Six days later, one hit the bow and exploded right under our forward gunnery post. Me and a guy named Emerson—didn't know him very well—both of us got pitched overboard by the concussion. Couldn't hear for a whole week after that explosion.

"Knocked me out, I guess. First thing I could remember was waking up, bobbing around in the water, and watching the Lucky Lou's lights steaming away from us. Ship like that can't stop on a dime, but I was scared we were gonna be left. Scared the sharks would get us. Scared that come morning Japanese planes would come and pick us off.

"Anyway," Dad continued, "me and Emerson were bobbing around in the ocean. We didn't talk much. Figure both of us knew we were goners.

"And sitting there, bobbing up and down in the water, I finally realized how stupid it was—what a waste of time and energy it was—to be scared all the time.

"Figure God put each of us here for a reason. Didn't know what I was here for. Still don't. Maybe it was to dig coal—keep people from freezing during the winter. Maybe it was to help in the war so we could live free, without some tyrant telling us our every move and every thought. Maybe it's to warn guys on an oil rig out in the ocean when a hurricane's coming and give them enough time so they can get to safety. Maybe it's something I haven't even thought about yet.

"Whatever God put me here for . . . well . . . when I've done all I can . . . when I've finished my job, or at least taken a good run at it, He'll call me home. No sense wasting my time worrying or being scared. Don't matter if I'm down in a coal mine or on the deck of a ship, dodging fire from an enemy plane or walking across a street in McAlester or Devlin Hollow. When it's time, it's time."

Dad leaned over so he could look Don square in the eye. "That's what I mean. The job is as safe as anything else. Now come on. We need to get to bed. Otherwise it's gonna be noon 'fore we get up. Clean miss Christmas morning."

As soon as they went inside, I checked the trash

can. Sure enough the raccoons had sneaked up from the back. They'd already been there. One had even crawled up and tried to pry off the lid. I guess the sound of Don's and Dad's voices had scared them off. But they'd be back.

I trotted to the house and made my rounds. When I got to Mom and Dad's window, I could hear whispering from inside. I stood on my hind legs and propped my front paws on the window ledge.

"Think they're asleep yet?" Mom asked.

"Don't know," Dad whispered. "I do know that we're supposed to go over and talk with the Devlins tomorrow. I don't want to fall asleep on their couch while we're visiting. If we don't get some sleep, that's exactly what I'm gonna do. You get the light. I'll get the chair."

The small light on Mom's side of the bed came on. Dad dragged a chair to the closet and climbed up on it. Then he started handing stuff down to Mom. She made two neat piles on the bed. When they were done, they took the things to the living room. Dad had closed the blinds on the north side of the house, so I couldn't see what they were doing. Didn't need to, though, 'cause I already knew.

Wrapped boxes and packages were already set beneath the tree. The things they were taking to the living room now, in the middle of the night, would be laid beside those packages. They would tell the kids that the wrapped stuff was from Santa's helpers; the unwrapped things, laid next to them, were the gifts Santa had left during the night.

Didn't really make sense to me, but that's the way they played.

Then I got to thinking about Mr. Devlin's rod and reel. I came *so close* to getting it for Don to use. Shame he took it back.

Then I got to thinking about Susan. I wanted her to be happy, too. Good as my nose was, I couldn't find a kitten any more than Don or Mom or Dad could. It was a shame. She was such a sweet and happy little girl. I sure wished—

The smell of raccoon swept the wishing and thinking from my head. I knew those rascals would be back! I hopped down from the porch and charged around the corner of the house. Raccoons were pretty easy to scare off, especially if I got to them before they found food. Once they dug something from the trash can and were eating, things wouldn't be so easy. They'd fight ya over food.

And to be quite honest, I didn't want to fight with a coon. Those guys were tough. Besides I was getting kind of sleepy myself. The sooner I scared them off, the sooner I could settle down for a little nap. There were four of them this time. But I startled them with my meanest, scariest snarl. They took off for the hill, and I trotted back to the porch.

I think I'd just dozed off when I felt the change. For Oklahoma it was a little different than usual. There was no wind. The cold crept across the valley, sliding and oozing as slow as cold syrup crawling across a cool pancake. It eased its way up our hill, swallowing the house in a chilly blanket. It was almost refreshing after all the warm weather we'd had. I managed to get in another nap before something woke me. I didn't know what it was—not at first. It was more of a sound than a smell.

I cocked one of my big floppy ears and peeked from beneath it.

Snow.

Gentle at first, it began to fall faster and faster until the air filled with the soft, drifting white flakes. It was pretty and peaceful as could be.

But there was something else. I couldn't tell

what. There was no smell. No sound. Cautious and curious, I made another round of the house. I couldn't find anything, so I made another round farther out.

Then I curled up next to the pile of wood that Dad and Don had laid on the porch. I enjoyed the snow. Marveled at the strange peaceful wonder that seemed to come with the tiny flakes as they began to hide the ground.

Chapter
21

Don had a vague memory of being halfway awake during the night. He'd sat up, pulled the quilt from the foot of the bed, and tucked it around his chin and over one ear. Seems like even before the cover had settled, he was asleep again. He'd felt warm and cozy and comfortable.

That's why the sudden jar was so irritating. He nestled deeper into the warmth of his quilt. The impact came again. Then again and again and again, almost as fast and unsettling as he imagined the machine guns on Dad's ship.

He lifted the quilt with an elbow and rolled over.

Susan bounced beside him on the bed. When she saw one eye looking from beneath the blanket, her smile seemed to brighten the whole room.

"It's Christmas!" she announced, bouncing even harder than before. "Wake up! Wake up! It's Christmas!"

Don moaned and curled back to his side, pulling the quilt to cover his head as he did. Susan just tugged it off, giggled, and bounced a few more times.

"All right. All right! I'm up." Don kicked his feet from beneath the quilt and pushed back the rest when he sat on the side of his bed. "I gotta go to the bathroom." Susan hopped from the other side of the bed. "You stay here."

Her bottom lip bulged out; then she grinned and crawled back on the bed.

"And don't bounce on my bed," he called over his shoulder.

A few minutes later, Don paused on the way back to his room. He tilted his head, focusing on the door to Mom and Dad's room. He heard voices, somewhere between talk and whispers.

"Awake?" he whispered.

"We're awake," Dad said.

Don nodded at the door and turned back to his room.

"Are they up?" Susan asked.

"Don't know. Be quiet. We'll go peek in their room and see."

Don knew Susan wouldn't peek in their room, any more than she would be quiet. But he told her that anyway. Just like he expected, the second he opened his bedroom door, Susan shot down the hall, flung Mom and Dad's door open, and darted inside.

She was already bouncing between them on the bed before he caught up to her. "Wake up! Wake up! It's Christmas!" she squealed.

Dad caught her in midbounce. Soon as he brought her down, he and Mom rolled, snuggling her between them. Dad snarled and growled as he smooched her neck and face. Mom tickled her sides and tummy. Susan laughed and laughed and laughed, until Don thought she was gonna wet the bed. Then they made room for him, and they all snuggled for a few minutes. Don enjoyed being in Mom and Dad's bed. It felt good to be with them. Felt good to act like a little kid again, safe and comfortable as it used to be when he was Susan's age. But it didn't take long for Susan to start wiggling.

"I want to go look under the tree," she said. "I want to play with what Santa brung."

Mom gave a little cough. "Brought."

Susan rolled over and frowned at her.

"Brought," Mom repeated. "I want to play with what Santa *brought*."

"Yeah." Susan's smile seemed to twinkle. "Me too!"

Don couldn't help but laugh at the mischievous grin on Susan's face. Dad tried to hold his laugh, but it came out as a snort. Glaring at both of them, Mom reached over and shoved his shoulder. Then she kind of punched him. Dad crawled, or with Mom's help half tumbled, out of bed, still chuckling to himself. "Let's all go see what Santa *brung*."

Susan started to follow. Dad snapped his fingers and pointed at the bed. "You stay put till I get my camera. I'll call you."

Susan didn't stay put. But Don held her at the door while Mom put her robe on. He didn't really hold her. They always fought and shoved, trying to see who could get out the door and to the Christmas tree first. Don was bigger and stronger, but he let Susan win.

Only he didn't let her win until he heard Dad call. "Ready!"

With that one word, Susan sprinted down the hall, darted across the living room, and slid on the carpet, stopping in front of her pile of presents. Don was right on her heels. Only he didn't slide to a stop in front of his pile. He just sat down because it was easier on his knees.

He held up the first knit shirt and smiled when he looked at it. Then he held up the second. His smile was even bigger because he noticed the folded pair of wheat jeans beneath the shirts. He looked at the second shirt and laid it aside. When he picked up the wheat jeans, he noticed a note pinned to them. Only he didn't read it.

That's because, as he lifted the jeans, he saw the high-top Converse All Stars. Don's eyes flashed so wide he was afraid they might pop clean out of his head. He snatched the jeans from the floor and held them up to stare at them.

Susan had her *Far Cheesy* game on the floor beside her. She picked up the Raggedy

Ann doll, hugged it, then set it aside to open her paper dolls and start putting the different dresses on them.

Mom was sitting on the couch, with her knees tucked under her so she could watch Don and Susan.

Don held the shoes beside his face. Dad's flash made him blink. Then he mouthed the words, "Thank you. Thank you. Thank you."

Mom and Dad both smiled.

Then they started on the packages. In a matter of minutes, the whole floor was covered with paper. Susan had some school clothes, a new pair of shoes, a pink sweater, underwear, and a new nightgown. Don added a dress shirt and two pairs of blue jeans to his pile. When he put his new pajamas down, he remembered the note on his wheat jeans. He dug them from the pile and read:

Dear Don,

I know you wanted some of these. If you manage to make it through October without getting grass stains on them, or tearing holes in the knees from playing

football with the guys, maybe I can talk
your mom and dad into getting you a
couple more pairs.
    Love,
    Santa

Again Don glanced at Mom and Dad. And again the flash went off, leaving a blue dot in front of his closed eyes, before he could mouth, "Thank you."

Mom and Dad opened their presents. Dad seemed right proud of the Barlow pocketknife. Mom loved the little silver necklace that Don had wrapped in the small box. She even got up from the couch to give him a hug and kiss him on the cheek.

But when she unwrapped the package that Dad gave her and held up the new nightgown, her eyes flashed big around as baseballs. It was frilly and lacy, almost as short as one of Don's shirts.

"I can't wear this," she gasped.

Smiling, Dad juggled a hot flashbulb from one hand to the other before he could set it down on the coffee table. "It's not for running around the house in," he explained. "You can put your robe over it." Mom's face turned red.

When everyone was through opening packages, Mom started gathering the wrapping paper. Dad got a few pieces and wadded them into tight balls that he laid in the fireplace. "Don," he called without looking up. "Why don't you put on your old tennis shoes and go bring in some kindling? It's getting a little nippy in here."

Mom stuffed her wrapping paper in the trash can beside the TV. "Susan, get your shoes on. You can carry the kindling while Don gets some logs." Then she turned to Dad. "Delbert. Come in the kitchen and help me a minute. I need you to hold the baster while I turn the turkey."

Susan slipped on her shoes and waited for her older brother.

Don held the front door for Susan and followed her out. She didn't pick up any kindling from beside the door. Instead she rushed to the steps and swooped up a Raggedy Andy doll in her arms. Don glanced right, then left.

There . . . beside the wood pile . . . was a

bright, shiny metal tackle box. It was open. There were two fold-out shelves with compartments. A different plug or lure was nestled neatly in each section of the top row. In the bottom was a stringer, three packages of hooks, and . . .

Chapter

here sure was a lot of falling going on around here. First Mom fell on the couch last night. Not plopped. Not sat. Fell!

Then Don looked in that metal box and fell down on his knees. He didn't kneel, one knee and then the other. He dropped like a rock.

It's a wonder his chin didn't hit the box. I had to squeeze between Mom and Dad at the end of the porch to get a good look.

At first I thought there might be a snake or something in the box. That's 'cause he moved so slowly, reached down so cautiously and carefully I was afraid something was fixing to bite him. Then when he pulled that bright silver, shiny fishing reel from the box . . . Well, the look on his face . . . the happy smell that came from him . . . the way he held it . . .

I couldn't keep my tail from wagging. It was swinging back and forth so hard that Dad finally stopped shooting pictures, reached down, and shoved my rump out of the way so it would quit whacking him and Mom.

Happy filled the crisp winter air. Even the few flakes of snow that fell couldn't stop it. Happy came from Don, Mom, and Dad. When Susan came to look at what Don held, the happy smell from her joined all the others. She even leaned over and kissed her big brother on the cheek.

Then with her doll tucked under her arm, Susan walked past him and looked at the far side of the pile of wood. She walked to the far end of the porch and then hopped off the side and walked to the big wood pile in the yard. She went to the pickup, opened the door, and held it while she searched under the seats. It took her a while, but when she came back, she leaned over and looked under the porch. Then she came to the front and peeked under the steps.

And with each place Susan looked, each searching, expectant glance at a different place, the smell of happy seemed to fade, leaving only the fresh, crisp smell of the snow to fill the morning air.

The shiny reel that Don clutched against his heart began a slow fall, inching downward until it finally dangled from one hand at his side. Dad swooped up the flashbulbs from the porch and shoved them in his pocket. Mom wiped her eyes with the sleeve of her robe. All four of us followed when Susan went to look in my doghouse and then opened the door to the little shed.

Don stood there, watching. Then he looked down at the reel.

I knew what he should do. I could smell that Don knew, too. Only it was hard.

Susan quivered and shook. I couldn't tell whether it was from the cold or from something else. Still she kept searching. She looked at the back door. She looked under the wash table where Dad left the coal dust when he came home from the mine. She even looked behind the big stump where I usually hid Red's and my bone. The snow was clear up to my dew claws, so deep that it sneaked over the tops of her shoes. I could hear her teeth chattering. Still she kept looking. Searching.

Don stopped and stared down at the reel again. My tail wagged when I smelled that he didn't only know what he *should* do—he knew what he *wanted*

169

to do. When I nudged his hand with my nose, he looked down and grinned.

"Quit cold-nosing me. You think you're Santa or something? I'm going." He spun and trotted toward the front of the house. Right before he stepped up on the porch, he turned and gave me a funny look. Then I could hear him muttering to himself, "Can't believe I'm talking to that dog like he knew . . . what . . . what I was thinking . . . like he . . . hmm . . ."

Don was sitting on the front porch when we came around the house. He held something behind his back. With his other hand, he motioned to Susan.

"Come here," he called in a whisper.

Her eyes flashed. Quivering and shaking all over with the cold, she bounded up on the porch and raced to him.

"Santa left something else for you. Guess you didn't see it."

He brought his hand from behind him and handed Susan the bright, shiny silver Zebco reel. She looked at it a moment.

"No. That's what *you* wanted," she said, trying to hand it back to him. "That's what you told Santa in your letter."

"That's right," Don agreed. "That's what I told Santa. But I wanted it for *you*. So you and I could go fishing. Only thing, I forgot to ask him for a rod to go with it." He slapped his forehead with the palm of his hand. "Dumb me. I should have put that in my letter. Didn't even think about it. But I've got some money saved up to get a new blade for my mower. It's almost enough for a new rod. You can use one of my rods until we can get—"

"No," she said, pouting. "It's what you wanted. It's yours."

Don shrugged. "Okay. If you don't believe me, read the note he taped on the bottom."

Susan turned the reel over. There was a little piece of red paper taped to the bottom that read, "To Don."

"It says, 'To Don.'"

He shrugged. "Turn the note over."

Susan's mouth fell open when she lifted the little piece of red paper. "It says, 'To give to Susan at Christmas.'"

"See. I told you so."

Susan frowned at him. "But you don't ever let me go fishing with you."

"Well . . . uh . . . that's because you were too little. You're bigger now. More grown-up. I figure you're old enough you won't be yakking all the time and scaring the fish off. And . . . well . . . and," he stammered. "And if we move to Texas, I won't have Kyle to go fishing with. And whether we move or not, I still think you are old enough to start catching fish."

"But *you* wanted it." Still bouncing up and down like mad, Susan's bottom lip stuck out.

"Now what in the world would I want another rod and reel for?" Don forced a laugh. "I've already got two rods and reels. Why would I want three? No way anybody could use three reels. It's yours. Honest!"

Don had sure been letting some stinkies lately. But this lie had kind of a nice aroma to it. Only trouble, now Mom was using both sleeves of her robe to wipe her eyes. Dad stood behind her and lifted the bottom of her robe to wipe his eyes. When she felt the cold air, she glanced over her shoulder. She didn't pull away until he was done.

"It's freezing out here," she said, clearing her throat. "Susan and I are going to get dressed, put on some dry shoes and socks. Delbert, why don't you and Don get the fireplace started?"

"Can I come in, too?" I asked with my best wag. I even perked my ears.

Nobody seemed to notice. But when Don picked up his armload of kindling, Dad opened the door for him. And when Don held the door open with his foot for Dad to bring the logs in, I slipped in between them.

Now this was Christmas! Happy house. Happy smells. Me curled up by the fireplace, waiting for them to start the fire—one happy dog.

The boys hadn't even put down their firewood, when Mom called from the other room. "About got the fire started? We need to get some of the chill off the house."

Chapter
23

Don hardly noticed how chilly the house was. But when Mom called, he realized how bad his toes were hurting from tromping around in the snow. He thought about offering to help, but Dad was right particular about his fire-starting. The paper had to be just right. The kindling had to be laid on top in a precise manner.

Besides that, Frank was in the way. He had his ears perked up, kind of standing right next to Dad on the hearth. It looked like Dad had enough help, so Don went to his room to put on dry socks and his new tennis shoes. When he finished lacing his Converse All Stars, he stood and looked down at them. He wiggled his feet and tried to turn his ankle. They felt *great*. The most wonderful shoes he ever had.

When he got back, Dad and Frank were

still getting the fire ready. Without looking Dad pointed up at the mantel. "Hand me the matches, Don. Would you please? We'll have this baby roaring in no time."

Careful not to crunch Dad's fingers or Frank's tail, Don stepped to the hearth and reached up to get the big box of matches. He handed them to Dad. That's when he noticed Frank.

Ears perked up and tail swinging, he leaned against Dad. Pushing him away with his elbow, Dad reached for a match. But before he could even get one out of the box, Frank shoved back against him even harder than before.

"Get back, dog," Dad growled, shoving him away. "What in the world's wrong with you?"

Dad pulled a match from the box, slid the box closed, then . . .

Right as he was about to strike the match against the rough strip on the side of the box, Frank reached out a paw and knocked the box clean out of Dad's hand.

"What in the world's wrong with this dog?" he snarled. "Stealing a fishing rod, now he's pawing at me like I was a bone he'd buried or something. We might need to take him to the vet in McAlester. He's acting weird."

With that Dad put both hands on Frank's shoulders and shoved him clean off the hearth. He struck the match on the side of the box. Frank bounded back toward him, but Don got there first.

"Wait!" Don said, grabbing Dad's arm. "Dad, wait. Frank sees something. He's smelling something."

Dad turned to frown at his son. Don nodded toward the bloodhound. "See the way his ears are up. And his tail. It's not wagging like he's happy. He's on to something. You know, like it wags when he hits a trail."

Dad rocked back on his heels. Don knelt beside him and tried to see where Frank was looking. Nothing moved. There wasn't a thing in the fireplace, except for paper and kindling. Don glanced at Frank again. Frank looked up. All three of them heard a faint scratching sound.

"Alice," Dad called. "Can you fetch me the flashlight?"

It took Mom a minute or two to get there.

When she saw Dad lying on his back, staring up into the fireplace, she didn't even have to ask. She did anyway. "Bird?"

Don figured the same thing. Last spring two starlings had gotten in the chimney. They were trying to make a nest or something. Mom had held the front door open while Susan held the back door. The second starling never would fly out. Dad finally had to catch it with a towel and pitch him out of the door to get rid of him.

Dad took the light, clicked it on, and shined it up the chimney.

"Not a bird."

"Let me go get your gloves," Mom said. "Could be an opossum or a raccoon. Those things can really bite."

"I can see the tail." Dad's voice was kind of muffled 'cause he was so far into the fireplace. "Not an opossum tail. Not a coon." He made a grunting sound when he stretched one arm up into the chimney.

"*Oh . . . my . . . gosh!*"

Mom, Susan, and Don took a step back. "What is it?" All three asked at the same time.

Dad didn't answer. He put the flashlight beside his head. He held something in both hands as he made grunting and moaning sounds as he wriggled out of the fireplace. When he sat up, he held whatever was in his hands out to Susan. Her eyes lit up the whole room. The chill in the house that Don had felt just moments ago was gone.

Susan took a little gray kitten from Dad. She snuggled it against her heart as she swayed gently from side to side.

"Santa knew." She sniffed. "He knew."

Chapter

Susan called her Ashes.

She snuggled her kitten and hugged her and smiled till I thought her face was gonna crack. The little beast didn't struggle or try to scratch. She just snuggled right back.

When Susan wasn't watching, Don and Mom looked at Dad. Dad and Mom looked at Don. Then Dad and Don looked at Mom. Then. . . .

Everybody looked at me!

I shrugged my ears. "Don't blame me. I didn't do it!" I even thumped my tail on the floor. They kept staring, and I knew that even though I told them, there was no way I could make them understand.

We ate Christmas dinner. Mom fed me some meat and dressing, and two hot rolls all covered with that delicious gravy. Susan fixed a bowl of milk for Ashes.

When they finally let me out, I raced around the house, trotted up the leaning willow tree, hopped to the shed, and then stepped to the roof. I smelled and sniffed every inch of the way as I went.

After making four or five treks across the roof and circling the chimney a few times, I still couldn't smell a thing. No kitten. No people. No nothing. At the chimney, I stopped and looked up. Maybe the stupid thing fell from a tree branch that hung over and managed to land . . . There wasn't a tree branch within yards of our chimney.

Don opened the door for me when I scratched on the screen. I curled up in front of the fireplace, staring at it and wondering how in the world—

Suddenly something climbed on my back. Little paws made about five circles before they stopped, and I could feel the kitten lie down. Then she started kneading with those sharp little claws. I cringed and flinched a little, but really 'n' truly it wasn't all that bad. Ashes finally settled down, and both of us took a nap.

"Guess we don't have to worry about Frank eating the cat while we're off at the Devlins," Dad said.

It was dark when they came home. Ashes was curled up on a couch pillow. Guess she was too young to know that she wasn't supposed to get on the furniture. There was a lot of talk and excitement about the new job, about moving, and especially about the two thousand dollars a month that Sam Devlin and his company were going to pay.

Dad reminded them that Sam told him the oil business was either "bust or boom." Right now it was booming. There was plenty of money. But in a year or two . . . who knew?

Mom and Don both said that the money was nice, but the *nicest* thing of all was Dad wouldn't be down in some mine.

Mom let Susan take Ashes to her room. Once sure they were tucked in and quiet, she came back and sat between Don and Dad on the living-room couch. Each asked the others *again* if they were the one who found the kitten and hid her in the chimney. And after each swore that they didn't do it, they all turned on me!

"Had to be Frank," Dad said. "He's the only one left."

"I don't think so," Don spoke up. "I watched him this morning. He climbed up the willow and onto the roof. You know that certain way his tail gets to going when he smells something, and how his ears perk up?"

"Yes."

"Didn't happen. He went all over that roof and around the chimney. I don't think it was him. I don't think the cat climbed up there. I don't think somebody carried her up there. If Frank could have smelled the cat, or smelled where she came from, he would have backtracked the thing."

"Maybe he couldn't smell with the snow on the roof," Mom suggested.

Don shook his head. "No. I was with him last winter when we had that big snow. Bet there was eight inches of snow on the ground. We were walking up past the lake and his old tail got to switching. He sniffed his way to this pile of snow. Not a track going in, none coming out. When he was about three inches from the pile, it exploded like somebody dropped a cherry bomb in it. This rabbit came flying out and took off. I don't think the snow bothers his nose one little bit."

Dad nodded his agreement. "I've heard that a bloodhound can even smell stuff that's down under the water." He sighed and glanced up. "Reckon we might never know where that kitten came from. But I still think it's him. He brought Mr. Devlin's rod and reel home, 'cause he knew Don wanted one. Why wouldn't he bring a kitten home for Susan?"

Mom reached across Dad to the end table beside the couch. She patted the black book that she took with her every Sunday when they went to church.

"Can't remember the chapter and verse, but I do know it's in the Book of Matthew in the New Testament." She sighed and touched the black book again. "I never can remember the exact words, either. But Jesus told his disciples that 'if you have faith as a grain of mustard seed, you can move mountains.' I guess if that little faith can move a mountain, it doesn't take much to move a kitten."

They looked at the book, looked at one another, and then took one last look at me. Then Dad wrapped his arm around Don's shoulder and hugged him so hard I thought Don's eyes were gonna bug out.

"When you get to be my age, you'll look back on stuff you've done. If you're like me, you'll think about all the stupid, dumb decisions you made—the things you did that you wish you hadn't or could go back and change. Other things—even after it's done and you've had plenty of time to think it over—you'll never know whether what you did was right or wrong. And seems like, least of all, you'll remember a few of the good things you did.

"What you did with Susan . . . well . . . you know . . . giving her your reel . . . I hope you're wise enough to remember *that* as one of the good things. I don't know when your mom and I have been more proud of you. It was . . . what you did was—" He broke off, then smiled. "As soon as I get my first paycheck, we'll get you another rod and reel. Promise."

Don shook his head. "I really don't need one. Right after I handed it to her, there was a little twinge inside. Just a little thought about how bad I had wanted it. But the look on her face and the good feeling I had inside chased it away. I'm kinda looking forward to teaching her how to fish."

"We'll get a new rod and reel for all three of us." Dad chuckled. "From what I've heard about those new spinning reels, Susan will learn how to cast it real quick. But it'll still take the whole family to bait her hook and take the fish off."

They let me out one more time before they went to bed. And one more time, I climbed to the roof to see if I could smell something.

It was a good Christmas—good for all of us—but . . .

I never did figure out where that darned kitten came from.

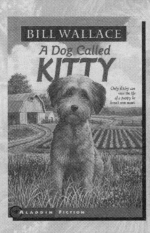

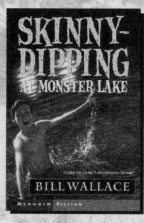